THE
MAGNIFICENT
MUMMY MAKER

THE
MAGNIFICENT
MUMMY MAKER

ELVIRA WOODRUFF

AN
APPLE
PAPERBACK

SCHOLASTIC INC.
New York Toronto London Auckland Sydney

ISBN 0-590-45743-8

Copyright © 1994 by Elvira Woodruff.
All rights reserved. Published by Scholastic Inc.
APPLE PAPERBACKS is a registered trademark of Scholastic Inc.

12   8 9/9

Printed in the U.S.A.   40

For Melissa Good and Melissa Kulp,
whose magnificent mummy
gave me goose bumps and this story
E.W.

THE
MAGNIFICENT
MUMMY MAKER

CHAPTER ONE

My name is Andy Manetti. I have been alive for ten years, and in all that time I have never done anything magnificent. I didn't think I could, so I usually didn't try. Jason, my ten-year-old step-brother, on the other hand, has been doing magnificent things since the day he was born. He is so magnificent that my stepmother, Marie, can't bear to part with anything her son puts his hand to. A perfectly scored spelling test that Jason had taken in the third grade is hanging on the bulletin board in our kitchen, even though Jason is now in the fifth grade.

"Jason has an incredible memory, as most gifted children do," my stepmother always says when she shows people the paper, along with all of Jason's other magnificent test papers hanging on the board. A few of my best efforts are tacked up alongside of these, but next to his one hundred percents, my seventy-fives and seventies look awfully ordinary. Jason, it seems, is "gifted," not ordinary like me, and it's beginning to make me sick!

It's a waste of time for me to do a lot of studying for tests, because no matter how hard I study, I know I'll never do as good as Jason does. I didn't even bother opening my math book for the chapter test last week. I opened my box of baseball cards instead.

"Andy, aren't you supposed to be doing your homework?" my dad asked when he came into my bedroom.

I shrugged and looked down at my collection of rookie cards. Dad sat down on the edge of my bed, his leg brushing up against Rickey Jones.

"You don't want to end up like me, do you?" he asked. "Going out and breaking your back every day, just to keep a roof over your head? If you study now, you can make something of yourself. You don't see Jason fooling around every night in his room, do you?"

I shrugged.

"No, you don't," Dad went on. "Because Jason knows how to study, how to apply himself." I groaned and looked at the wall.

"Listen, Andy, I know it hasn't been easy for you, living alone with me all these years. Maybe I haven't paid as much attention to your schoolwork as I should have, maybe things would have been different for you if . . ." His voice trailed off and he didn't say anything for a long time. I just kept staring down at my cards.

"I just want the best for you, Andy," Dad finally said. "And let me tell you something else." He leaned over and lowered his voice. "Jason may be smart, but you're no dummy, either. You can pull these grades up if you want to. All you have to do is to try. Jason wants those A's and he wants them real bad. If you want them bad enough, you can get them, too."

"Right," I muttered, after he had left the room. "All I have to do is want great grades and like magic my report card will be instantly transformed." I looked down at my math book on the floor and back to my baseball cards.

I never did open my math book that night. It seemed so useless, and besides, my mind was on other things. I couldn't help thinking about what my dad had started to say, about how things would have been different if . . . if my mom hadn't died when I was a baby. That's what he meant. I spent the rest of the night wondering what it would have been like, and how different my life might have been if my mother had lived. Would I have turned out differently? Would I have gotten better grades? Would I have been gifted, instead of ordinary? Would I have turned out like Jason? Agh! That thought was enough to give me nightmares.

The next day, when Miss Haverly, my social studies teacher, told our class about this latest project, Ancient Egypt, I just shrugged and looked out the window. I had no way of knowing that with this project, I would be transformed from ordinary ten-year-old Andy Manetti into "Andy Manetti, the Magnificent Mummy Maker!"

"All the fifth grades will be studying ancient Egypt, and each class will work on a display to represent that amazing civilization," Miss Haverly explained to the class, her face flushed with excitement. This was Miss Haverly's first year teaching, and whenever she talked about a new project, her eyes lit up and she blushed a deep pink.

"Today we'll be reading about how the ancient Egyptians viewed death," Miss Haverly was saying now. "I'll be handing out study sheets that show you some of the symbols and script called hieroglyphs that the Egyptian writers used. These writers were called scribes. We'll be going over the sheets tomorrow, and then I want you to study the symbols so that we can use them correctly in our display. Ancient Egypt was an amazing . . ."

I yawned as Miss Haverly's voice became a jumble of background noise. I wasn't thinking about ancient Egypt. Ancient Egypt seemed boring. I was thinking about my baseball card collection, and wondering if Max Silvestri would trade his Ken Griffey, Jr., for a Will Clark. Now that was interesting.

I have been collecting baseball cards for almost two years and I have the biggest collection of anyone I know. I didn't go out for Little League this year, because I'm not a very good player, not like my stepbrother, Jason. He's a star player, and I cringe at the thought of trying to compete with him on a ball field. I'm just glad that Jason hasn't decided to collect baseball cards.

Miss Haverly's voice came gently floating back to me. "As all the fifth grades will be working on similar displays, we've decided to invite parents to a special Ancient Egypt night, here at school. It will give them a chance to see all the work that you've done. The best work will be selected for the school's art show this spring. Now, there are a number of projects that you can choose from for your display," she told the class. "We'll be making coiled pottery out of clay, replicas of pyramids out of Styrofoam, landscape paintings of the Nile, and more."

I closed my eyes and thought about Jason. I knew that his gifted class would also be making a display. I could just imagine the magnificent pot, pyramid, or picture that Jason would come up with. And I knew that it would probably be so good that it would win a prize in the art show and Jason would come home with yet another ribbon. One more magnificent thing to stick up on the bulletin board.

Why me? Of all the stepbrothers to get in the

world, why did I have to get stuck with Mr. Gifted! And if that's not bad enough, he has to be the same age, in the same school, and now we both have to work on the same boring project.

"Hey, Andy, wake up, and pass these down," a familiar voice suddenly broke into my thoughts. I opened my eyes to see my best friend, Keggan McGrath, who was sitting in front of me, handing me a stack of study sheets.

"I'm sorry, Keg," I whispered, taking a sheet and passing the rest to the girl behind me.

"Now, I want everyone's attention as I tell you about the most exciting part of our study." Miss Haverly's voice was soaring. "We will be taking a trip to the Barton Museum of Fine Arts," she told the class. "Some of you may have already heard of their Secrets of the Nile exhibition that is there this month." At this announcement, a collective sigh of pleasure circulated around the room. I shrugged. I didn't see anything exciting about a museum. I think museums are boring. I wished we could visit a ballpark instead. Now that would be exciting.

Miss Haverly's eyes grew wide. "We're going to be able to get a chance to see some magnificent artifacts that were created in Egypt centuries ago," she continued. "After our visit we will be using all the information we've gathered, and we'll be ready to create a magnificent display of our own. The very best work will go on to be displayed in the museum's Children's Gallery."

Miss Haverly beamed with the exuberance of hope. I sighed the pained sigh of the hopeless. I didn't expect to create anything magnificent. I shoved the paper full of strange symbols into my social studies book without even looking at it. I closed my eyes again and tried to think about my baseball cards, but couldn't. All I could think about was the big boring museum we'd be visiting, with rooms full of boring old stuff. Then we'd all come back to school to work on some boring display. I was about to yawn when I heard Katie Donnalson ask, "Miss Haverly, will there be any mummies at the museum?" I opened my eyes on hearing Miss Haverly's reply.

"Yes, there is a mummy in the exhibit."

"How old is it?" Kevin Munsa wanted to know.

"The museum's brochure said that it is believed to be over two thousand years old. I think that now would be a good time to look at our fact finder sheet on mummies," she said. "Katie, will you please read the first paragraph." I shuffled through my papers and found the one on mummies. There was a picture of a mummy wrapped and un-wrapped. Wrapped looked weird, but unwrapped looked weirder. There was this old bony person that was almost a skeleton. I followed along as Katie began to read:

"The Egyptians believed that life after death was very much like life on earth. They protected and preserved their dead for this reason. The pyramids were used to protect the body. Body preservation, a process known as mummification, was developed around twenty-six hundred B.C. Mummification might take as long as seventy days. First the brain was removed from the body, often through the nostrils.

"Oh, gross," Katie cried.

We all began to laugh and hold our noses. Miss Haverly waited for the commotion to die down before telling Nelson Walters to continue reading.

"Next the other vital organs were taken out. They were put in sealed, airtight jars. Then the body was allowed to dry out for forty days. The Egyptians used a salt compound called natron to do this. The body was then treated with molten resin and oils, and finally wrapped in linen bandages."

"All right, you can stop there," Miss Haverly said. "That's enough about mummies for now. You'll all get to see one next week, and we'll be talking more about them then, so hang on to your sheets. Now let's turn to page fifty-nine in our books."

"A mummy." I whispered the word under my breath, as I mechanically turned the page of my social studies book. I felt a slight breeze sweep over the back of my shoulders, and the hair on my arms stood up.

What would it be like to see a real mummy? I wondered. Would it smell? Would we be able to touch it? A strange feeling of excitement tinged with fear crept over me as I thought about a body that was thousands of years old. Miss Haverly's voice came back to me as she began to read aloud.

"Since the Egyptians believed in an afterlife, everything that the dead would have needed to survive in real life was placed in the tomb, such as food, clothing, jewelry, and weapons. In this way, the Egyptians felt their happiness was ensured in the afterlife."

Miss Haverly paused. "Any questions or comments?" she asked.

"If it were my tomb," Keg spoke up, "and they wanted to ensure my happiness in the afterlife, I would need a TV, my three kittens, my fish, Floater, and a two-thousand-year supply of soda and potato chips."

Everyone laughed at this, even Miss Haverly.

"Well, Keg, I don't think television sets were found in any tombs from ancient Egypt, but everything else you mentioned probably was. They did place offerings of food and many other things in the tomb. And if they didn't use the real thing, they would use replicas. Let's all turn to page sixty-two to see an example of this."

I turned the page and looked down to see a model ship filled with little toy Egyptian men rowing. It reminded me of my pirate ship fil!ed with action figures.

"This is a replica of a boat outfitted with slaves and supplies. It was found by archaeologists in a tomb dating back over three thousand years ago," Miss Haverly told us.

"I wonder what it's like to be a mummy in a tomb for three thousand years?" Keg said. As we spent the rest of the period talking about tombs and mummies, I began to realize that ancient Egypt wasn't going to be as boring as I thought it would be. For the rest of the day I thought about the mummy we were going to see in the museum on Tuesday.

I had a hard time falling asleep that night. My dad and Marie were going over bills at the kitchen table, so the TV wasn't on. The house was quiet, too quiet I thought, like a tomb. I suddenly felt chilled and pulled my sheets up to my neck. This only made me feel worse as I imagined myself wrapped from head to foot in bandages, like a mummy. I threw off the sheet and buried my head under my pillow.

I finally fell asleep, but I had the strangest dream. I dreamed that all of my baseball cards had turned into mummy cards! Instead of a picture of a player on each card there was a picture of a mummy!

When I woke up the next morning, I leaned over my bed and pulled up a box full of cards from the floor. I sighed with relief as I ran my fingers over the familiar faces and figures of the ball players printed on my cards.

I tried putting the unsettling dream out of my mind. I tried to forget about mummies, altogether, but couldn't. I spent the entire week thinking about the visit to the museum, wondering and worrying. I didn't know why, but it was as though an alarm would go off in me at every mention or thought of the word *mummy*.

CHAPTER TWO

On Saturday morning Keg called on the phone to ask me if I wanted to come over for breakfast. His older sister, Megan, had tc make a special meal for a nutrition project she was working on for school.

"I don't know," I answered. "What are you having?"

"Well, I'm not sure," Keg said. "The last time Meg cooked us supper it looked like something that came out of a mummy's tomb. It looked like ancient meat loaf."

"How did it taste?" I asked.

Keg laughed. "Do I look dumb enough to eat ancient meat loaf? I fed it to the kittens under the table. But Meg can make great desserts. She's making apple crisp this morning." I thought about the ancient meat loaf and took a whiff of the air. My stepmother, Marie, was making French toast. New French toast. So I decided to skip Meg's breakfast.

After saying good-bye to Keg, I walked into the kitchen and sat down at the table.

"Andy, hurry up and eat your French toast before it gets cold," Marie called from the stove. Marie is not like the witchy stepmothers you read about in fairy tales. She rarely yells and usually finds a nice way of telling me to do things. Marie loves to wear lots of jewelry. Big jewelry. She's got four rings on one hand and two on the other. She also likes long dangling earrings, and she's always wearing them, even when she's in her nightgown. I guess some people would call Marie fat, but I don't think of her as fat. I think of her as big. Everything about Marie is big, even her smile. I like her smile a lot.

I don't remember my real mother. She died when I was only two months old. My dad and I lived alone until he married Marie four years ago.

The best part of living with Marie is that I don't have to go to day care or to my aunt's house after school, because Marie is always home. She takes care of my new little sister, Winks. I never thought I'd like having a baby sister so much, but Winks is special. She has this funny look, as if she knows exactly what I'm saying to her, even though she's only a baby.

Winks is a great listener. Sometimes I baby-sit while Marie is doing housework. I take Winks out to her little red swing in the side yard. My dad hung the swing from a low branch of our old oak tree.

Winks loves to swing. I like to kiss her neck before I push her into the air. Her neck smells like flowers and baby powder. Winks's real name is Vanessa, but to me Vanessa sounds like an old lady, not a six-month-old baby.

Her favorite toy is a plush pink pig, with one eye that always seems to be winking. Once I caught her trying to wink back. So now, every time I see her, I say, "How's it going, Winks?" and she smiles. She doesn't smile when Jason says, "Hi, Vanessa," which brings us to the worst part of living with Marie — Jason, her son from her first marriage. Jason was living with his dad, but decided to come live with us this past summer. It was the worst summer of my life.

"I got a ninety-six on my math test yesterday. Did I tell you?" Jason said as we sat at the breakfast table this morning. He looked over at my father. Dad's mouth was full of French toast, so he just nodded his head. But before Dad could say anything, Winks let out a loud burp from her infant seat. I grinned. Winks knows how to handle a braggart.

I didn't even know what a braggart was until Jason moved in with us. Marie had given me a calender for my birthday and it had a new word for every day of the year. Braggart was the word for February 25. It should have been the word for March 2, Jason's birthday. The definition says that braggart is someone who is always bragging and boastful. If the dictionary people had ever met Jason, I'm sure they would have put his picture next to the word.

"Almost half the class failed the test," Jason continued to brag. "There were only two scores above eighty."

"That's great, hon," Marie said, with a smile. "Keep it up, and you can become a mathematician someday."

"Or you could become some hot-shot accountant," Dad said. Jason beamed. "And you could build a big monster house over in Brently, and hire me to do the brickwork," Dad continued. "Hey, Marie, can you see me pulling up to Jason's mansion in the Chevy?" Everyone laughed at this. My dad's a mason, and the pickup truck that he drives for work is an old beat-up Chevy.

I shoved some French toast in my mouth and thought about my last math test. I had gotten a sixty-nine. It occurred to me that now would be a good time to change the subject, and I was about to mention how Winks was looking like a baby bald eagle, when Jason spoke up.

"So how did *you* do on your math test?" he nearly shouted across the table.

"Not bad," I mumbled.

"Not bad? Meaning a C or a D?" A mean little smile had crept onto his face.

"Almost a C," I whispered, looking down at my French toast.

"That means a D," Jason announced to everyone. I was hoping Dad wouldn't hear, but when I raised my head, I could see that he was looking straight at me.

"Andy," he said, "you're just not trying hard enough. You should be getting A's and B's, not C's and D's. I want you to go to college someday. If Jason can get good grades, so can you."

Isn't one Mr. Gifted in the family enough? I wanted to answer. But I didn't, for I could see the wrinkles forming on Dad's forehead. They seemed to be there a lot lately. I knew that he was worried about his job. My dad's got a bad back, and lifting block and hauling brick hasn't been easy. A couple of doctors told him that he should quit, but being a mason is all he knows how to do.

"If I had gone to college," Dad continued, staring off into space, "I could have gotten a degree in forestry and become a forest ranger. We could all be living in the Grand Canyon right now."

"Phil, you're such a dreamer," Marie said, shaking her head.

"I don't want to be a forest ranger," I complained. "And I'm glad that we don't live in the Grand Canyon. Who wants to live where they don't even have sidewalks? How would you be able to skateboard?"

"Andy, you're not getting this." Dad sighed. "You

16

don't have to be a forest ranger. You can be whatever you want, as long as you work hard and get good grades. Maybe if you thought a little less about skateboarding and a little more about your schoolwork, you wouldn't be getting D's."

I just sat there staring down at my French toast. I didn't look at Jason, but I could feel him grinning from across the table.

"What you need is a tutor," Marie suggested as she began feeding some yellow cereal to Winks. "You and Jason never do anything together. Maybe Jason could help. He could tutor you."

I rolled my eyes and groaned.

"It's either that or you'll have to ask about extra help from your teacher," Dad said.

I'll ask my teacher," I quickly replied.

Anything but Jason, I was thinking. Just then Winks reached for the spoon in Marie's hand, scooped a little fist full of cereal out, and shoved it into her mouth. Marie and Dad were dumbstruck.

"Did you see that, Marie?" Dad cried. "She fed herself!"

"Oh, my gosh! What a big girl!" Marie cooed. "What a good girl!"

I gave Winks a wink from across the table. Her new stunt couldn't have come at a better time, for Marie and Dad had forgotten all about my math test and were now preoccupied with their "good girl."

What a life Winks has, I suddenly thought. All she has to do is sit there and stuff some cereal into her mouth and she's accomplished this great feat! She didn't even get it all in her mouth, for a glob of it was sitting on her nose.

"Speaking of college," Marie said as she wiped at Winks's face with a washcloth. "I was reading in the paper about a seminar the community college is giving to teach people about color."

"Marie, even I didn't have to go to college to learn my colors," Dad said. "They teach you that stuff in kindergarten."

Marie shook her head. "This is something different. It's a color encounter workshop, where people can discover which colors define who they really are. From what the article said, we're all supposed to have certain key colors that correspond to our personalities. They call it being in a certain color zone."

"Take a look at your daughter," Dad said, pointing to Winks, who was busy smearing the yellow cereal over her chin now. "Wouldn't you say that she's definitely in the yellow zone?"

"Well, I guess you could say that she's got a sunny disposition." Marie smiled.

"And, Mom, you're in the red zone," Jason said. We all looked at Marie's hair.

"It was supposed to be auburn." She sighed. Marie had recently dyed her hair, and though it said auburn on the box, it had come out red on her head. "Besides, your color zone is supposed to define who you are, not just what you look like," Marie told us.

"I don't know, babe," Dad said. "I think Jason's right. I knew you were a red-hot mama the minute I laid eyes on you." He grinned, Marie blushed, and Jason and I made faces.

"Well, when I think of you, hon," Marie said, looking at Dad. "I think of brown."

"Brown? Why brown?" Dad frowned.

"Because you're strong like an oak, and you're so in touch with the earth," Marie said, smiling. Dad smiled, too. Marie was always coming up with corny stuff like that. I don't know why, but Dad seemed to like it.

"I guess brown doesn't sound so bad after all," he said.

"What about me?" Jason whined. "What color would I be?"

"When I think of you, Jason," Marie said, squinting her eyes. "I think of blue, blue-ribbon blue."

"Um, that's a good color for him," Dad agreed.

Well that was all Jason needed to hear. He puffed out his chest, as if he thought another ribbon were about to be pinned on him at any moment. I began to wonder what color they would pick for me. As I sat waiting, Winks began to squirm in her chair. Dad reached over to take off her bib, while Marie

19

unfastened the strap in her infant seat. Jason was busy staring at the blue ribbons on the bulletin board, and probably worrying that there wouldn't be room for another one. No one was thinking about my color zone.

I guess it was just as well, because I don't think they would have come up with a good color, anyway. I certainly wasn't blue-ribbon blue, we all knew that, or even brown like Dad. I wasn't strong or smart. I wasn't red or yellow, either. I was nothing. I was gray. I hate gray, but I bet that's the color they would have chosen for me.

I was sitting at the table feeling like nothing, when I heard the phone ring. Dad went to answer it.

"It's for you, Andy," he said. I walked over and took the receiver from him. It was Keg again.

"Well," Keg told me. "I finished breakfast and I'm still alive."

"How was it?" I asked.

"The eggs were green, some kind of parsley mixture, and the toast had a green mint spread on it. Eating green food the first thing in the morning is a disgusting way to start your day. Even the kittens wouldn't touch the stuff. I guess you were smart to stay home." We talked for a little while about what I had for breakfast, and then Keg asked, "Have you decided on what you're going to make for your special Egypt project?"

"I'm not sure," I whispered, walking into the hallway with the phone, so no one could hear me. "I have to wait and see what Mr. Gifted is making first. I don't want to do the same thing that he does, because his project is bound to come out better."

"It must be tough living with a Mr. Gifted." Keg tried to console me.

"You have no idea." I sighed.

"Well, I have an idea for the project, and it's something that Jason won't be able to do," Keg whispered excitedly.

"I'll never come up with something better than him," I groaned.

"Oh, yes, you will," Keg said. "This is one idea that even the genius won't think of. You're going to get an A for sure with this one."

I pressed the phone to my ear. The idea I had thought of was okay, but what I needed was something more than okay. I was hoping this was it.

"So go ahead, tell me. What is it?" I asked nervously. Keg's excited voice came back on the line.

"We can make a mummy," he whispered.

"You mean a fake mummy," I said.

"No, a real mummy," he said.

"A real mummy with a real dead body?"

"That's right," Keg whispered. "We can take a real dead body and turn it into a real mummy!"

CHAPTER THREE

"Keggan, are you crazy?" I whispered into the phone. "People can get put in jail for fooling around with dead bodies. Besides dead bodies give me the creeps."

"This one won't," Keg assured me. "It's so little it isn't creepy at all."

"A baby?" I cried. "Are you talking about a dead baby?"

"Who said anything about a baby?" Keg gasped. "I'm talking about a hamster."

"A hamster?"

"Yeah, my sister's old hamster, Wiley, died yesterday, and I was thinking that if you wanted to, we could try and mummify him."

"I guess that sounds a little better," I replied. "But how are we supposed to mummify him?"

"I could sneak some salt and oil out of the kitchen," Keg whispered into the phone. "And we've got a whole roll of bandages in the bathroom cabinet. What do you say?"

The thought of a mummified Wiley made me queasy. "I don't know," I replied. "It sounds good, but do you remember that picture in our social studies book, the one of the model ship? I was thinking that I could use my old pirate ship and some of my action figures."

"Okay," Keg said, obviously disappointed. "But if you change your mind," he whispered, "let me know. This could be the first mummy hamster in history."

"Sounds great, but I think I'll stick with the boat." Those were the last words out of my mouth when I saw Jason leaning in the doorway, obviously spying. He pushed his blond hair out of his eyes with a grin.

"What are you so happy about?" I asked, afraid that he might have overheard my plans, but of course he answered me in German.

"Mein Boot ist besser als deines," he said, with a smirk.

The gifted class was learning German and Jason was learning how to drive us all crazy by going around the house speaking nothing but German. There's something so obnoxious about the way Jason is always trying to show you how much he knows. He even made a long paper banner to hang over his bed. None of us could read it though, because it's written in German. He finally told Marie what it meant. Quiet. Genius at Work.

"That's great," I heard Marie say.

"No," Jason corrected her. *"Das ist sehr gut."*

Yuck, I thought.

But amazing as it is, we don't all feel the same about Jason's lapsing into his *"Das ist sehr gut"* routines. In fact Marie seems to love it! Her face lights up whenever she hears Jason utter something unrecognizable. Dad tries to smile, but you can see that he isn't too thrilled. I wish that Dad could be more honest about Jason. He must hate him as much as I do, but Dad won't let on. He just smiles and says nice things to Jason. He even upped Mr. Gifted's allowance after his last report card. The only thing he upped after my last report card was the number of TV shows I wasn't allowed to watch on school nights.

Jason returned to the kitchen now, and I heard him ask Dad if he could help him with a "special school project." I knew that it must be the Egypt project, though Jason wouldn't say. He was being so secretive, that later he locked himself and Dad in the garage, so they could "work in private." Sitting in my room, I could hear Dad's power saw start up.

Miss Haverly had told us that all the fifth grades could start on their projects over the weekend, or wait until Wednesday. We had no school on Monday due to a teacher's convention and would be visiting the museum on Tuesday. It figured that Jason was starting on his already. He probably wanted to be that much closer to another blue ribbon. That's how those blue-ribbon types are. As I listened to the power saw, I began to feel worse and worse.

Why didn't I think to ask Dad for help with my project? I was his real son, after all, not Jason. Why was I the one who was locked out? Just then Marie stuck her head in my room.

"Andy, you're so good with the baby. Will you watch her for me while I do my hair?" she asked. "You know how she hates the sound of the blow dryer. I'm going to take her shopping with me as soon as I'm through. I want to get her a new outfit to wear for your dad's birthday party on Sunday."

"Sure," I said as she placed Winks's infant seat down on my rug. Winks watched Marie go into the bathroom and shut the door. Then she looked at me and smiled. She likes it when I baby-sit for her.

"So, Winks," I said, leaning over to pull on her toes. "It looks like you're going shopping. I think you must be the world's best-dressed baby. Your mother sure loves to buy you stuff." Winks made a gurgling sound and blew a little bubble.

As I sat looking at her, I began to think about

my own mother. Ever since Winks was born, I've been watching her and Marie, and it makes me wonder.

"What do you think my mother was like?" I whispered, looking over at Winks and giving her toes another tug. "Do you think she was like your mom? Do you think she was constantly shopping for me and fussing over me? I've wanted to ask Dad about it, but I can't. He never talks about my mom. It's as if she never lived. Marie explained it to me once. She said that my mom's death is still too painful for Dad to talk about." Winks tilted her head. She looked as if she understood. So I went on.

"It's not painful for me, though," I said. "What's painful is not talking about it. I know I can never have a real mother, the way you have Marie. But sometimes I think about how good it would make me feel just to hear that my mom fussed over me and loved me the way Marie loves you and Jason."

Winks suddenly frowned.

"Oh, I know that Marie likes me," I told her, "but it's not the same. I'm not really hers. And I'm not smart like Jason or cute like you. You two even look alike with red cheeks and blue eyes and blond hair. Well, your hair has a ways to go," I said, rubbing the little bit of yellow fuzz on the top of her head. She seemed to like that. "You can see that your hair is going to be blond like Jason's, though," I told her. "My hair is dark brown, darker than Dad's and curlier than anyone's in our family. Come to think of it, I don't look like I even belong in our family."

Winks yawned at this, and although she seemed sympathetic, she looked sleepy, too. In fact, she was beginning to nod off when the sound of Dad's power saw, coming from the garage, suddenly startled her. She let out a little shriek.

I picked up the infant seat and began to rock her back and forth as I walked around the room. Winks would make a great astronaut. She loves motion, and it wasn't long before she had settled down and was happily sucking on her thumb. As we walked around the room, the sound of the power saw was replaced by hammering.

"What do you think they're making in there, anyway?" I whispered. Winks squinted as if she were thinking this over.

"Must be a pyramid," I told her. "I bet it's a big plywood pyramid. You know how Dad loves to make things out of plywood." Winks blinked in agreement.

"That's okay," I said, placing her infant seat back down on the floor and going over to my closet. "Mr. Gifted can go ahead and make the biggest and the best pyramid in the school," I told her. "I don't care because my project is going to be just as good this time or better." Winks looked as if she were really interested in seeing what my project was, when

27

Marie suddenly came in from the bathroom.

"Don't worry, I'll show it to you later on," I whispered in Winks's ear, before Marie picked her up. After they left, I closed my door and locked it, then I dragged my old toy pirate ship out of my closet and began looking for some action figures to go inside of it. I tried to pick the ones with dark hair, so they looked more Egyptian, though they were dressed in modern clothes. There wasn't much I could do about their clothes, since they were made of hard plastic that didn't come off, but I decided to make some new sails for the ship. I got out my markers and colored paper and my work sheets. After studying the hieroglyphs on the sheet, I was able to copy out the symbols that spelled my name. It took a long time because I kept making mistakes, and I wanted to get the sails just right.

This was one project that I was not going to be outdone in. Everyone had talked about pyramids and mummies, but no one had mentioned the models for the tombs. I hoped that mine would be the only one. The new paper sails came out better than I expected, and it wasn't long before I had them taped over the old plastic ones. I spent a long time going through my toy chest looking for things that I could place in the ship. I found some little plastic boxes and some string, and I even found some tiny plastic fruit, which had come from an old game. I carefully arranged my action figures so that they were sitting down. But they didn't look like they were rowing. I needed to find them some oars.

I ran into the kitchen and grabbed a box of tooth-picks from the cabinet. It took a long time, but I was finally able to place a toothpick in each of their hands. When I finished I stood back to give it a final look, and tried to imagine what it would look like next to the other projects on Ancient Egypt night. Not bad, I thought, not magnificent, but not bad. I hid the boat under my bed, where it would be safe from Mr. Gifted's eyes until Wednesday morning.

I spent the next couple of days fooling around with Winks and reading my study sheets on Egyp-tian writing. I had had such fun writing my name in the Egyptian symbols that I decided to make some tiny banners written in hieroglyphs, which I could hang across my boat. The more I studied my sheets, the faster I figured out the letters. What I hadn't figured out though, was what Jason was up to. He seemed to spend all of his time working on his project.

On Tuesday morning, my eyes popped open at the sound of my alarm going off. This is it, I thought. Mummy day! I leaned over my bed and pulled my blankets back to check on my boat. It was still there and still looking pretty good. I smiled as I quickly got out of bed. Maybe for once I had come up with a better idea than Mr. Gifted. I couldn't wait to see his face on Wednesday morning when he saw me walking out of my room with my boat.

It wasn't easy eating breakfast that morning. The food was all the right color (there wasn't anything green), but I was just so excited about my project and about going to the museum, that my stomach felt too fluttery to eat. I looked across the table to see Jason shoveling a fork full of pancakes into his mouth. He didn't seem nervous at all. It was then that I began to wonder again about his project. I still didn't know what it was, for he had sneaked it into his room from the garage, and his bedroom door had been locked all weekend. It suddenly occurred to me that his door might not be locked now.

My curiosity was getting the better of me. Jason had spent so much time working on his project. I just had to know what it looked like. I sat waiting for my chance, and it was only a matter of seconds before it came.

"Jason, will you feed the cat. I can hear her crying on the porch," Marie said. I sat silently poking my fork at my pile of pancakes. My heart began to race as Jason grumbled and then got up from the table. I held my breath and waited for him to walk out the back door onto the porch. Then I got up from my seat as normally as I could, and took a few giant steps into the hall. Marie and Dad were busy fussing over Winks.

Once out of sight, I bolted for Jason's room. My hand was on the doorknob, and it easily turned. It was open! I poked my head in the room and looked around. There was nothing on the bed or on the bookcase. I took a step inside, but stopped cold in my tracks. I let out a little gasp, before my mouth dropped open, for there on his desk sat his project, Mr. Gifted's incredibly magnificent project!

CHAPTER FOUR

Jason's project was not a plywood pyramid. Jason's project was a boat! A real wooden Egyptian-looking boat, with real material sails and wooden oars! It was better than anything I could have dreamed of making. Even his men were better, because he had made them out of clay and they weren't dressed in modern clothes. They looked like real little Egyptians. They looked magnificent. Once again Mr. Gifted had outdone me! He had taken my idea (for I was certain now that he had heard me when I was on the phone to Keg), and he had gone out of his way to make me look bad.

I quickly shut the door and dragged myself down the hall to my room, where I threw myself on my bed. He's done it again, I was thinking. One more blue ribbon for the blue-ribbon boy. I leaned over and lifted my blankets to take another look at my own boat. Suddenly it didn't look Egyptian at all.

It looked like an old pirate ship with action figures holding toothpicks. It looked pathetic. I slumped down onto my pillow.

"Hey, what are you doing back in bed?" Marie called as she passed my room. She was taking Winks into the bathroom across the hall to change her diaper. "Aren't you feeling well?" she called as she placed Winks on the changing table. I lay watching them through my open door.

"I'm just tired," I said limply. "Tired of Mr. Gifted, your wonderful son," I muttered under my breath. I closed my eyes and tried to think of something else, but all I could think of was that magnificent boat and how magnificent it would look on Ancient Egypt night with a blue ribbon on it.

"How can you be tired?" Marie said, coming into my room. "Didn't you sleep well last night?" She leaned over me, with Winks in her arms and put her hand on my forehead. I hate to admit it, but I like when she does that. I always hope that my forehead is really hot, and she'll say, "Oh, Andy, you poor thing, you're burning up!" But she didn't, because I wasn't.

"You don't have a temperature," Marie said, removing her hand. "Go and have another glass of orange juice," she suggested. "That will give you a little boost, but hurry because the bus will be here in ten minutes, and today's your class trip. You don't want to miss that, do you?"

I suddenly did want to miss it, more than she knew. The best part of going to school, was that we were in different classes. Jason went one way and I went the other. Today, we'd both be going the same way, to the museum. I dragged myself to the kitchen, where Jason was putting on his sneakers.

"What's wrong with you?" he asked, on seeing me slump down in my chair. I glared at him. Dad was about to say something to me, when Marie burst into the room, announcing that she had forgotten to make our lunches. Dad helped her make the sandwiches, while Jason and I collected our things before the bus came. Miss Haverly had suggested that we bring our study sheets on Egypt, since it would be a long bus ride, and we could go over them once more before we got to the museum.

Keg was not on the bus. Oh, no, he's probably sick, I thought to myself, as I laid my book bag on his empty seat. If the museum was going to be any fun at all, it was because Keg and I would be going together. When we finally arrived at school, I dragged myself to our classroom and sank down in my seat. Miss Haverly was bustling around the room, taking attendance and getting ready for the trip. Everyone was squirming in their seats and whispering excitedly about the museum.

"Oh, Keggan, I'm so glad you won't be missing the trip," I suddenly heard Miss Haverly say. I looked up to see Keg come walking down the aisle.

"Where were you?" I whispered, after he had taken his seat.

"Meg made breakfast again this morning," he told me. "This time it was mostly purple. I only ate a few mouthfuls and then I got really sick and missed the bus, so my mom had to take me. She said that Meg is just 'trying to be creative with her cooking, and that we have to be patient.' I said she's trying to poison us, and I'm not eating anything that my kittens won't eat. Cats aren't good at being patient, but they're good at staying alive." We sat discussing cats and purple food for a while longer, and then Miss Haverly announced that the bus was here to take us to the museum.

We all went outside again to get on the long, gray bus with the words *Streamline Coach* printed on the side. I was relieved that I was able to sit next to Keg. At least something was turning out right. I looked up toward the front of the bus and saw Jason sitting with his gifted class. It was then that I told Keg all about my pathetic boat and Jason's masterpiece.

"What a creep," Keg kept saying, which somehow made me feel better. After that we talked about his plans to mummify Wiley and build him a tomb.

"My sister buried him out in the backyard near the septic tank," Keg told me. "She only dug down a little, because it's smelly over there. So it won't be hard to dig him up. I'm not going to mummify him until I have his tomb built though, and for that I need a pyramid. My dad says that the shape of the pyramid has something to do with its power. So even if I put Wiley's mummy into a cardboard pyramid, it might still be able to protect his body."

We weren't so sure about this, so we took out our study sheets to see if it mentioned the powers of cardboard pyramids. While we were searching through the sheets, I had an idea.

"Let's use the hieroglyphs and write a message to put in Wiley's tomb," I suggested. Keg hadn't studied the sheets the way I had, and I ended up doing most of the work, but I didn't mind, because it took my mind off what had happened at home with Mr. Gifted.

We finished, just as the bus pulled up to the museum.

"Time to see Mr. Mummy," Keg whispered as we stepped down the bus steps. At the mention of the word *mummy,* a wave of goose bumps popped up on my arms.

CHAPTER FIVE

Walking through the Barton Museum's Egyptian exhibit was like walking back in time. As Keg and I followed the guide through stone archways, past giant pillars and statues, it felt as if we really were in ancient Egypt. It was a little scary, but exciting, too, and definitely not boring.

The first glass display case that Keg and I looked in had a pair of sandals made completely of gold. There was a big gold bracelet and earrings to match. Outside of the case was a little plaque that said the gold came from the tomb of a queen from the 18th Dynasty. Seeing all that gold jewelry made me think of Marie. She would have liked the 18th Dynasty.

We also saw tiny carved figures of frogs, turtles, and crocodiles, which the guide told us were made to "invoke the aid of helpful gods." I thought Winks would have liked those. In another glass case, a little blue hippopotamus stood all alone. The museum's guide came up beside us and began to tell us about the little hippo.

"The hippopotamus," the guide began, "was a mythical enemy of the king. Figurines such as this were made to neutralize the destructive forces in nature believed to be working against the kingdom." As I stood listening, I wished I could take the little hippo home with me so I could neutralize the destructive force at work in my kingdom, namely Mr. Gifted.

Next we looked at a board game called *tjau*, which we found out meant "robbers." There was a small drawer in the board, where the game's pieces were stored. These were little green shapes, but what I liked most were the little throwing sticks called *dejeba* or "fingers." These were made of red-stained ivory and were carved at one end with the head of a jackal and at the other end with a fingernail. We listened as the guide explained how the obstacles in the game were equated with the hazards of the afterlife, and knowledge of its rules helped the newly dead to enter the underworld. He explained that it would be like our having to win at Monopoly in order to gain entrance to the underworld. Keg and I looked at each other and laughed. We both knew that Keg would never make it to the underworld, because he always loses at Monopoly, and I always win.

I was leaning over the case, thinking about my speedy entrance into the underworld, when Miss Haverly and the guide came up beside me.

"All right, everyone," the guide called. "I'd like you all to wait here, and as soon as the group ahead of us has moved on, you can follow me into the antechamber to the left. Through that archway lies the mummy of a priestess who was believed to have lived and died over two thousand years ago."

"Oh, so it's Miss Mummy," Keg said as we stood waiting. "Just think, Andy, if we do a good job, Wiley could end up here."

"We?" I said. "What do you mean 'we'? I told you I don't want to mummify your sister's hamster."

"I know," Keg whispered. "But you can't turn in your boat, not after what you told me about Mr. Gifted's masterpiece. The mummy part won't be so bad, really. Besides you don't have any other ideas for a project, do you?"

I had to admit that I didn't. And I couldn't imagine coming up with anything as magnificent as Jason's project. But would I really have to mummify a hamster, just to get a good grade? Not only did that make me feel creepy, but I was also beginning to wonder what Miss Haverly would think. I wanted to ask her about it, but Keggan swore me to secrecy. He was convinced that if the other kids found out about it, there would be a room full of mummified pets. My reminding him that no one else in our class had a pet who recently died did little to sway him. The Mummy Wiley was to remain a top secret.

As we followed the guide through the archway, I suddenly stopped thinking about Wiley's mummy and began to think of the mummy we were about to meet. I had to adjust my eyes to the darkened room. A hush fell over our group, as the stillness of the room overtook us.

I know it sounds funny, but there was something about the quiet of the space that was almost loud. It wasn't like the thinking kind of quiet in a library, or the cozy quiet in a house when a baby is sleeping. It was another kind of quiet altogether. It was a forceful quiet, cold and final, and powerful. It was so powerful, I could hear my heart jumping in my chest.

"This chamber," the guide's voice suddenly broke through the stillness, "is a re-creation of an actual chamber in a tomb near the Valley of the Kings. The falcon panels that you see lining the walls actually lined the enclosure wall of the pyramid complex." As I walked past them, I stared at the tall stone panels, and recognized some of the hieroglyphs carved into the stone from the symbols on our study sheets.

I turned my head to the center of the room, and then I saw it. The mummy! It lay in a long glass enclosed case that was bathed in a white light from above. I held my breath as we stepped up to the case. I was relieved to see that the mummy was still wrapped.

My eyes traveled over the ancient linen bandages, stained yellow and brown, that bound the mummy's lower half. The upper half was covered with a carved wooden mask.

"She must have had some big feet," Keg whispered, pointing to the mummy's wrapped feet. Miss Haverly shook her head, and a number of girls began to giggle.

"Actually the women of ancient Egypt were about the same size as the women of today," the guide said. "In bandaging the body, thick pads of linen were placed over the feet to prevent any injury when the coffin was set on end so the mummy could be displayed in an upright position." Keg was shaking his head, and I knew he was picturing Wiley on display in an upright position.

"This mummy's feet were probably no bigger than your teacher's," the guide told us.

"Do you think she painted her toenails, the way Miss Haverly does?" Melissa Hubbard wondered aloud. This brought on another chorus of giggles as everyone looked down at Miss Haverly's red painted toenaiils, which were visible through the cutout toes of her shoes. Miss Haverly blushed a deep red, almost as red as her toenails, at all the attention suddenly focused on her feet.

"That's a good question," the guide said, smiling.

"Actually the Egyptians invented many cosmetics. I'm not sure about nail polish, though. Our next stop is the gift shop, and you can probably find some books there on the subject."

At this suggestion, everyone followed the guide as he began to walk out of the room. Everyone except me. I needed to have another look.

"Come on, Andy." Keg was pulling on my sleeve. "Let's see what we can buy in the gift shop. Maybe they have some chocolate mummies we can buy for the trip home." Keg is always thinking of his stomach.

"I'll be right there," I whispered as I slowly walked around the case. Keg shrugged and followed the rest of the class into the gift shop. I was staring down now, into the case. The top half of the bandaged priestess was covered in a carved wooden mask. The wooden arms and hands were in a crossed position over her chest. A delicate necklace was carved around the neck and painted blue and gold.

I felt a chill run through me as my eyes traveled upward to the mummy's masked face. The nose was long and straight, and the lips were half smiling. The mummy's eyes were big, with shiny black pupils and blue-green eyebrows. Streaks of blue green were painted on either side of each eye.

They aren't real eyes. This is not a real face, I had to keep reminding myself, for though I knew better, I couldn't shake off the feeling that the face staring back at me was alive!

I was leaning over the case with my hands pressed to the glass, when suddenly I felt a strange, tingly sensation travel through my fingertips to the rest of my body. I could feel my face flush with heat, and my teeth were chattering. I was feeling hot and cold at the same time, and then I didn't feel anything at all. It was as if a sudden wind had swept through me, blowing out all my senses.

"Andy," I could hear Miss Haverly's voice calling. It sounded very faint at first, but then grew louder. "Andy, we've got to stay together. We're all going to the gift shop now."

"Oh, right," I mumbled, looking up to see Miss Haverly waiting for me. My teeth stopped chattering just as suddenly as they had started, and I began to feel like my old self again. I stole another glance at the mummy before moving away, but somehow it looked different. It seemed so lifeless now, and I had the strangest sensation. It was as if I had just taken a long drink and was feeling quite full!

CHAPTER SIX

I felt a little odd when I woke up on Wednesday morning. For a moment I had that same weird feeling, as if there were someone else inside of me besides me. I was going to talk to Dad about it at breakfast, but I took one look at Jason and knew that he'd make fun of me if he overheard, so I said nothing. I had other things on my mind, anyway. It was Wednesday, project day, and I was suddenly without one, and without a clue as to what I would make.

I watched with envy as Jason carried a big shopping bag out of his room. He had stapled the top shut, but I knew that his boat was inside. And I knew that he probably wanted to have a grand unveiling for his class. I decided that the best place for my boat was under my bed, and that's where I'd left it. I was hoping Jason wouldn't notice its absence as we walked to the bus stop, but, of course, he did.

"So where's your project?" he asked as we stood waiting for the bus.

"I've come up with a better idea. I'm going to work on it in school today." I shrugged. He smirked. I shrugged some more. We both knew I wasn't kidding anyone. I sighed with relief at the sight of the bus coming down the street.

"So, have you changed your mind about Wiley, yet?" Keg greeted me as I sat down beside him in our seat at the back of the bus.

"Oh, not that again," I groaned. "Keg, I'm depressed enough without having to think about pulling old Wiley's brain out through his nose."

Keggan made a face. "Shhh, will you keep your voice down," he muttered. "Besides, we don't have to work on the mummy part until we have the tomb done."

"Thanks, but no thanks," I replied.

"But what will you do for your project then?"

"I'll come up with something."

"Suit yourself, but you're missing a great opportunity. I'm sure Wiley will be the only hamster mummy in the exhibit."

"You're probably right about that," I agreed. "But I thought the book said that it took seventy days to mummify a body. You won't have seventy days to finish him."

Keg took a quick look around to see that no one was listening. "I've thought of that already," he whispered. "The book said that it took seventy days to mummify a human body, but Wiley isn't a human body. Wiley is a hamster body."

"Well, how long does a hamster body take?" I asked.

"I'm not sure," Keg said, shaking his head. "But with that little bit of a body, I'd bet it wouldn't take more than seven or eight hours. So I can wait and mummify him when I'm through making his tomb. But the tomb's got to be just right," Keg was saying. "Because I have to make sure that his *ka* is happy."

"His what?"

"His *ka*," Keg repeated as he reached into his book bag and pulled out the book he had bought at the museum. "I was reading this last night. Listen to what it says. He looked down at the opened book and began to read:

"The Egyptian believed that he had two separate, indestructible souls. When he died, his *ba*, or ghost, left his body in the form of a bird. His *ba* maintained contact with his body in the tomb and his *ka* in another world. His *ka* was his divine nature, his vital force, and it stayed with him in life and followed him to the tomb before arrangements were made for passage into the other world. If the circumstances in death were not pleasing to the *ka,* it could wait in the body, before escaping into another vessel."

We spent the rest of the bus ride talking about Wiley's *ba* and his *ka,* and I still had no idea what I was going to make for my project.

It wasn't until later that morning, when Miss Haverly said, "All right, everyone, you can begin work on your projects now," that I found myself busy making something.

It was the strangest thing, because even though I went up to a roll of brown paper and cut off a sheet about six feet long, I still hadn't a clue as to what I was going to do with it. It wasn't until I began cutting into it, that I realized I was cutting out the shape of a mummy!

Usually when I try and make something in school, I get nervous about it not coming out good, and so I make a lot of mistakes, but this project was different. I wasn't nervous at all and I didn't seem to be making any mistakes. As I cut through the paper, I had this tingly feeling running through me, and little shivers running down my arms. I kept on cutting. I looked down at the scissors in my hand. I could see myself cutting out the shape of a mummy, but I couldn't feel myself doing it. Something strange was going on. When my mummy was cut out, even Miss Haverly was surprised.

"Andy, what a beautiful job! Did you trace that?" she asked. I stood back, shaking my head no, and looking at the perfectly shaped mummy.

"I'm not finished," I heard myself say. I spent the rest of the period working on my project. It was as if I were in a trance. I didn't have to copy from a book or a picture, as most of the other kids did. I knew, or my hands knew, exactly what to paint. I gave my mummy bright blue eyes and deep red lips. I painted her mouth closed. She was neither smiling nor frowning. The expression on her face was that of supreme calmness. On her head I painted a black-and-gold wig. Using colored foil paper, I cut out delicate-looking jewels and glued them around her neck to form a dazzling necklace. On her arms I gave her colorful tattoos — a bird and a fish.

I've never been very good in art. My paintings usually look like blobby messes, sort of the way Winks looks after she's had her face in her cereal. But suddenly I found myself painting like a real artist! There wasn't one blob on my paper. On the lower half of my mummy I painted gold and silver hieroglyphs. The paint seemed to flow off of my brush effortlessly, as it had never done before, and I began to mix colors until the mummy was glowing with crimsons, burnt oranges, sea blues, and deep purples.

I suddenly realized that something inside of me

was making me a great artist. I had the power to make something incredible! And I knew it had something to do with the mummy in the museum. I looked around the room to see what everyone else was making. There were some good things being made, nice pyramids, tombs, and pictures of the Nile, but nothing could compare with my mummy. With each brush stroke, she blossomed into an amazing piece of art. It was unlike anything I had ever done or ever hoped to do. It was "magnificent!" That's what Miss Haverly said, as she and the rest of my class gathered around me and my mummy.

"Oh, Andy," Miss Haverly gushed. "I never knew you were so, so — so gifted!"

I felt strange, definitely strange. I knew that something had happened to me when I had leaned over the mummy's case, but I didn't know what. On the outside, I looked like the same ordinary Andy Manetti, but on the inside, I felt so different. It was as if seeing the mummy in the museum had shaken something inside of me.

What was going on? I wondered. Was I going crazy? How could someone who's been dead for two thousand years do anything to me? And why did I feel so full? As if I had eaten a big meal, when I had barely touched my breakfast.

CHAPTER SEVEN

Imagine yourself making the most magnificent thing you've ever made, the most magnificent thing anyone in your entire school has ever made, and you'll know how I was beginning to feel. My whole class was standing around my mummy, and it was as if they were all in a trance. "Wow!" "Awesome!" "Great!" they cried as they stood staring. I was staring, too, for it was hard for me to believe that I had anything to do with creating something so "wonderful."

"Wait until your dad and Marie see it," Keg said, coming up to stand beside me. That thought made me smile, but then I had another thought. Wouldn't it have been great if my real mom could have seen it? I had never made anything this good before and I suddenly wished she could have been alive to see it.

As I stood there, I realized that the strange full

feeling I had first experienced in the museum was suddenly gone, and I was beginning to feel like my old self, except that now, no one was treating me like my old "ordinary" self.

"Truly magnificent," Miss Haverly cooed over and over to me, until a few of the kids began to chant, "Manetti, the Magnificent Mummy Maker."

Keg came up and whispered in my ear, "Why didn't you tell me you were planning on doing something this great? This even tops Wiley! Andy, you're amazing!"

And that's pretty much how everyone began treating me after they looked at my mummy. Miss Haverly even hung it in a place of honor next to the chalkboard behind her desk. Then she sent messages to the art teacher and the principal's office, to let them know about the "magnificent mummy in room 210."

I was enjoying all the attention so much, that I stopped wondering how it happened. I knew of course that I could never make something so wonderful all by myself. Something else was going on here, but I didn't have time to figure out what. Our classroom was suddenly filling with spectators, who had come to see and admire "Manetti's masterpiece."

"Stupendous!" Mr. Supps, our principal, bellowed as he stood before my mummy.

Stupendous? I couldn't believe my ears. No one

had ever called anything I had done stupendous.

Mr. Supps continued. "We've never had a student display such, such . . ."

"Creativity!" Mrs. Foley, the art teacher, gushed. "Andy, this is really incredible. I had no idea you possessed such talent, such skill, such vision."

"I've heard of such cases, though it's very rare," Mr. Minrow, the guidance counselor, added in a serious tone. "The child appears to have no extraordinary talent, tests at grade level, or below grade level, and then quite suddenly, perhaps due to some emotional shock, the latent talent is awakened within." Everyone turned to look at me. I closed my eyes and yawned. All this awakening was making me sleepy.

The grown-ups stood whispering as they watched me return to my seat. I sat down and gave a little wave. They nodded their heads and smiled, as if Leonardo da Vinci himself had waved to them. I picked up my pencil, and a hush fell over the classroom. Everyone's eyes were on me as I began to scribble on the cover of my math book. It was my usual kind of scribble, with a lot of squiggly little lines looking like worms. Mrs. Foley came down the aisle and looked over my shoulder. She stood shaking her head.

"Amazing perspective," she whispered. Then she returned to the front of the room.

Stacy Brinkly shot me a dirty look. Stacy Brinkly

is the best artist in the fifth grade. Everything she makes gets fussed over and hung up. I squirmed in my seat. Stacy Brinkly squinted her eyes and chewed on the end of her pencil, as she looked from me to my mummy. I knew what she was thinking. She was thinking that something must be going on for me to have made such a "masterpiece," and I knew she was right.

It didn't take long for word to get out. At lunch everyone was talking about "Manetti's Magnificent Mummy." Kids were suddenly offering me their best food, cupcakes, and bags of chips. Later in the hallway, two girls stopped to ask me about how I made my mummy. I saw Jason standing by the water fountain watching. I wondered how he felt, now that he had a winner for a stepbrother, instead of a loser. By the frown on his face, I guessed he wasn't too happy. Welcome to the club, I thought.

When I returned to our classroom, a group of kids were standing around my mummy and they began to clap when I entered the room. For some reason I thought of my mother again. I wished she could see my mummy, too. I wished she could know that I had made something so good.

"All right, let's settle down," a deep voice commanded. I was startled to see a strange, dark-haired man sitting at Miss Haverly's desk. His face was round like a little soccer ball, and he had a brown mole on his cheek. Then I remembered Miss Haverly telling us that we would have a substitute for the next three afternoons, while she attended a special teachers' workshop.

As everyone began returning to their seats, I sat down and looked at the substitute teacher, and I couldn't help wondering about his mole. I wondered what it would be like to have one myself. I wondered if he shaved it? Was he born with it? Or did it just start growing one day? I was hoping he would tell us about it.

"My name is Mr. Gaven," the substitute finally said, his lips turning down into a frown. "And I do not intend to spend the next three afternoons baby-sitting. You are fifth-graders and you had better begin to act like fifth-graders. When that bell rings, you are all to find your seats and zip those lips. Understood?"

Everyone hurried to their seats. No one said another word, but we all understood. We understood that Mr. Gaven was probably the crabbiest substitute teacher living on the planet, and that the next three afternoons were not going to be fun-filled. I decided that now would not be a good time to ask him about his mole.

"I see you're studying Egypt," Mr. Gaven said, turning toward my mummy. "That's an incredible representation. Your teacher didn't do it, did she?"

"No," Keg spoke up. "The Magnificent Mummy

Maker did. Andy Manetti made it." Then he turned around and pointed to me. I cracked a little smile, but Mr. Gaven did not smile back.

"You mean you and your parents made it," he said, looking me over before returning his gaze to my mummy.

"No," I told him. "I made it right here in school, this morning."

Mr. Gaven's frown grew frownier (if that's possible.) He stared at the mummy and then looked back at me, as if I were lying.

"Well, Mr. Magnificent," he sniffed. "Maybe you'd like to show us how talented you are in math. Everyone open your math books to page forty-six, and Mr. Manetti, you may put the first problem up on the board for us. The fellow in front of you can do the second and the girl in front of him the third."

I hated the way he called me "Mr. Magnificent." He almost sounded jealous. Why was he treating me so mean? I wondered as I dragged myself up to the board behind Keg. I suddenly knew how Jason must feel, when I call him "Mr. Gifted." But I wasn't like Jason. I wasn't bragging or showing off. I had simply done something wonderful, probably the only wonderful thing I would ever do in my life. I cringed at the sight of the math problem on the board. So much for wonderful.

Going up to the chalkboard to do a math problem

can be a nightmare for someone like me, someone who's terrible in math. It's bad enough to feel stupid when you're alone in your seat, but to have to put your stupidity up on the board for the whole class to see is like slow death. And I always die at the chalkboard. As far as humiliation goes, it's right up there with striking out on a ball field.

I was thinking about this as my fingers tightened around a piece of chalk, and then I thought of my mummy and the wonderful morning I had spent with everyone thinking I was so magnificent. A "star player." If only I could fool them a little longer. Instead of giving up on the math problem, as I usually did after two or three tries, I stuck with it, determined to get it right. I could hear Keg moaning beside me. He was no better at math than I was.

"All right, people, let's finish up," Mr. Gaven finally barked. I rushed to do the last bit of addition as he tapped on Miss Haverly's desk with a ruler. I bit down on my lip nervously, waiting to hear if I had struck out as usual.

"The first problem is correct," Mr. Gaven announced. "You may take your seat." I couldn't believe my ears! I had gone up to the board, and I hadn't died! Suddenly I imagined myself on the ball field. It was a night game. The lights were flashing, the fans were going crazy! "Another home run for Manetti!" I could hear the announcer cry. "Yes, they're calling him Manetti the Magnificent, and you can certainly see why. He's impossible to beat!"

"I said you may take your seat." Mr. Gaven's crabby voice broke into my daydream.

"Oh, sorry," I mumbled, coming out of my daze and walking back to my seat.

Thank you, Miss Mummy, I thought as I looked over at my mummy hanging next to the chalkboard. I knew, of course, that she didn't give me the answer. Or did she? Was it because I forced myself to take the time to figure it out, or was it the mummy working some kind of magic? Whatever it was I was feeling great. Poor Keg, on the other hand was striking out, and Mr. Gaven was not about to let him slink back to the dugout unnoticed.

"Since when is seven times three twenty-two?" Mr. Gaven bellowed.

"Since today?" Keg replied in a small voice. Everyone laughed at this, everyone except Mr. Gaven. I was beginning to think that he never laughed. As he went up to the board to correct Keg's answer, I gazed over at my mummy. She certainly was beautiful. My eyes traveled over the intricate hieroglyphs painted in dazzling colors, and I smiled. In the background I could hear Mr. Gaven going through Keg's problem, step by step in a tired, crabby drone.

How does a person get so crabby? I wondered

as I continued to listen. And was there ever a time when he wasn't crabby? Was he a crabby baby? Did he ever do anything silly? Did he ever laugh?

As I sat staring into my mummy's deep-blue eyes, I began to wish that Mr. Gaven would do something silly, like trip and land on the floor. Maybe that would shake him out of his crabbiness, I decided. No sooner had I wished this than the strangest thing happened.

"What is six times five?" I heard Mr. Gaven ask as he towered over Keg.

"Six times five is . . ." Keg was hesitating, afraid to make another mistake. "Thirty-five," he finally sputtered.

On hearing this reply, Mr. Gaven took off for the board, and in his hurry he bumped into Jack Carlton's desk, causing him to trip and fall to the ground.

Everyone laughed until they heard Mr. Gaven's voice.

"Would someone care to tell me what's so funny?" he barked.

The room grew deadly silent, but as Mr. Gaven stood up and faced the chalkboard, his dark hair slid over on his head and was hanging over his left ear. Mr. Gavin was bald! And the hair he had on his head was fake! A flurry of giggles rose up, and soon the whole class was laughing again.

My eyes traveled from Mr. Gaven and his lopsided hairpiece to the dazzling mummy behind him. I felt the hair on my own head stand up, for the mummy seemed different somehow. Why hadn't I noticed it before? I wondered. It was something about the expression of her face, her smile. I didn't remember her looking so satisfied.

CHAPTER EIGHT

I think I was the only one in the room, besides Mr. Gaven, who was not laughing. I was too confused to laugh, for I suddenly realized that my magnificent mummy was more than a paper mummy. I knew then that she was as powerful as she was beautiful. She had read my thoughts, I was sure of it, for as I was making my wish I was looking directly at her. And she was smiling such a strange smile. Was it really the same smile I had painted on her? Or had it somehow mysteriously changed?

"Stop," I whispered, under my breath, staring straight at my mummy. "Let things go back to normal."

I reached over in my seat and grabbed the back of Keg's shirt. He was doubled over laughing.

"Keg, listen, this is serious," I whispered, pulling him toward me.

"If it's a hair joke, I'm ready," Keg gasped, between laughs.

"Keggan, get a hold of yourself," I pleaded. "Something strange is going on."

"Tell me about it," Keg cried, looking back at Mr. Gaven, who was frantically adjusting his hairpiece.

"Strange and scary," I said, pulling Keg back toward me.

"Scary? What's scary?" Keg had stopped laughing for a minute. I quickly told him all about my wish and the mummy's magic.

"Don't you see," I whispered. "I could never have made that mummy all by myself. You know I'm not that good in art. It has to have something to do with that mummy I saw in the museum and the strange way I was feeling after I leaned over the case."

"I don't know," Keg said, shaking his head. "I think you're getting a little carried away with all this mummy stuff."

"What about her smile?" I asked. "Doesn't she have a strange smile on her face? Look for yourself."

"Andy, you're sounding a little loony if you ask me," Keg said, turning back around in his seat. I was about to say something else, but the room had grown quiet, as Mr. Gaven was now standing stony-faced, with his hair in place, before us. For the remainder of the period everyone sat waiting for his hair to slide on his head, everyone but me. I was almost certain that without me and my mummy, Mr. Gaven's accident would have never occurred. Keg, on the other hand, was not convinced.

"Andy, you don't really believe that mummy magic stuff, do you?" he asked, after the bell had rung and we were walking together to the art room.

"How do you explain Mr. Gaven's falling down?" I asked.

"That's easy," Keg said. "He walked right into Jack's desk. Anyone would have fallen down if they had done that. Although, their hair wouldn't have slipped across their head that way." Keg was laughing again.

I shook my head as we walked into the art room. I was relieved that the period had ended, and I had a chance to leave the room and get away from the mummy. I was so confused about her I didn't know what to think.

"Oh, Andrew," Mrs. Foley exclaimed as I took my seat. "I'm so glad to see you!"

"I'm glad to see you, too, Mrs. Foley," I mumbled.

"Andrew, it's not often that we have a truly magnificent work of art in our midst here at Jefferson Elementary. Won't you share your masterpiece with the rest of the school?"

"Share her? You mean like cutting her up into little pieces?" I asked.

"Cut her up! Oh, heavens, no!" Mrs. Foley cried. "I would like you to bring her here into the art room for the day, so that she can be displayed for all the art classes to see."

"Well, I guess so," I muttered. Mrs. Foley stood looking at me.

"Oh, you mean, now," I said, frowning.

"Yes, right now," she said, smiling. "Take Keggan with you, and he can carry one end and you can carry the other. We wouldn't want a wrinkled masterpiece, would we?"

I was beginning to wonder if we wanted a masterpiece at all. It took all of my courage to walk back into Miss Haverly's empty room and go up to the mummy. I was suddenly afraid to touch her! We walked back to the classroom, and I stood on a chair so I could reach her.

"What are you so worried about?" Keg asked when he saw me hesitating. "It's not real. It's only paper."

"That's what you think," I whispered nervously as I tried to work up the courage to touch her.

"Andy, feel this." Keg sighed. "What do you feel? Is this paper, or isn't this paper?"

"It's paper, but it's powerful paper, I'm telling you."

"All right, then if it's so powerful, prove it," he said.

"How?" I asked.

"If the mummy can direct Mr. Gaven to do something, it should be able to direct anyone. What about me?" Keg asked.

"You?"

"Sure, it's the only way you can prove it to me. I'll try my hardest not to do one weird thing all through next period. You and your mummy can go ahead and work your magic, and we'll see what happens. Just don't make me kiss Melanie Spadoni, that would be too weird." He laughed.

I looked down into the eyes of the mummy. My hands trembled as I felt the paper rustle in my fingers. "Okay, Keg," I said as we walked back into the art room. "But don't say I didn't warn you."

CHAPTER NINE

Mrs. Foley had a special bulletin board in the art room. Across the top of the board AMAZING ART was spelled out in glittering gold letters. Each week, the best pictures were hung there. Stacy Brinkly's stuff always made it up, and I had seen Jason's pictures up there a number of times. Even one of Keg's pictures had been up once. It was a painting of his fish, Floater. None of my pictures ever went up on the board. None of my stuff was ever "amazing" enough, until now.

We hung the mummy with tape from the back. Mrs. Foley insisted that we not make any holes in the paper with tacks. "It would be a sin," she said, her voice filled with reverence.

Keg and I stepped back from the bulletin board and looked up at the mummy to be sure she was hanging straight. I quickly turned away, for the sight of her made me shudder. Suddenly her deep-blue eyes seemed real. I could feel a kind of force coming through that paper form, the same force that I had felt coming through the mummy in the museum. It was then that I realized that the mummy in the museum had somehow transferred this force to me and it had gone from my hands into the paper mummy. Now all I had to do was prove it to Keg.

"Andrew's mummy should be an inspiration to you all," Mrs. Foley was saying as she passed out jars of paint and paper. "I want everyone to take note of his superb use of line, his attention to detail, and his wonderful feel for color. Notice the masterful balance of textures in his brush strokes, and the playful use of design. It's so free flowing, so spontaneous. This work is truly a celebration of the imagination." Mrs. Foley sighed heavily as she stood gazing at my mummy. Then she turned back to the class.

"Now, I want you all to celebrate your imaginations with mummy paintings of your own," she said, her voice rising with enthusiasm. "Think of the masterpiece you are about to create. Be free, be spontaneous, and don't get paint on the floor."

Everyone opened their jars of paint and then picked up their brushes. I looked over at Keg, who was sitting beside me in the next aisle. He looked at me and crossed his eyes and stuck out his tongue.

"Oooo, it's working. It's working," he whispered,

rolling his head around. "That old paper mummy is making me so weird. Ooooo."

"You'll be sorry," I whispered back.

"Sure, sure." Keg grinned. We both grew quiet as Mrs. Foley came down the aisle. She was stopping at each desk, offering suggestions and checking to see that kids weren't getting paint all over. As she stood with her back to us, leaning over the desk in front of Keggan's, I knew what I had to do. I looked at Keg out of the corner of my eye. He was outlining a mummy form on his paper with black paint. I lifted my head and, looking my mummy in the eye, I made my wish.

Make Keg do something weird. Something that everyone will notice, I wished.

Turning to look back at Keg, I saw that my wish had instantly come true! Keg had dipped his paint-brush into a jar of green paint and, as he lifted his brush out of the jar, Frank Sabatino suddenly sneezed beside him. It was such a loud sneeze that Keg turned to look and, as he did, he swung his brush, and a big glob of green paint went flying off his brush and hit Tony Hague on the side of his head!

My eyes darted back to my mummy, and I gasped to see the smile on her face! It was that same strange smile.

"Stop!" I whispered under my breath. "Make them stop!" I focused my eyes on the mummy's eyes and would have sat there staring longer if the noise around me hadn't broken my trance. The class was in an uproar as they watched Tony dip his brush into his jar of orange paint and flick a glob back at Keg.

"Tony! Keggan! Stop this instant!" a frantic Mrs. Foley was yelling as she grabbed the brush out of Keg's hand.

"It . . . it was an accident," Keg stammered, a glob of orange paint dripping off his chin.

"He did it first," Tony cried, smearing a green streak across his cheek with his fingers.

"You can save your explanations for Mr. Supps," Mrs. Foley snapped as she marched them to the front of the room. The class was instantly silenced by the crackle of anger in her voice and the mention of Mr. Supps, our principal.

Poor Keg looked back and blinked several times as he was led across the room to the door. I tried to get his attention, but he was staring down at the floor. Then just as they were about to leave the room, I saw him pass under the mummy and his mouth dropped open. He had suddenly understood what had happened. He turned to me and was about to say something, when Mrs. Foley dragged him out of the room. When I looked back at the mummy, she was smiling that strange smile, looking as satisfied as ever!

I spent the rest of the period copying the hieroglyphs I had painted on my mummy into my notebook. Mrs. Foley didn't seem to mind what I did.

"Feel free to express yourself, in any way that you wish," she said as she stood over my desk. "Inspiration can be such a fragile thing. I want you to just go with the flow."

I didn't know about "going with the flow." The only place I wanted to get was to the bottom of this whole thing. I was afraid to wish for anything else that period, and my mummy didn't smile again. Keg wasn't smiling either, when I saw him later that day on the bus for the ride home.

"I'm really sorry," I said, sitting down beside him. "I didn't mean to get you in so much trouble. How much trouble are you in, anyway?"

"Oh, it wasn't too bad." Keg shrugged. "Mr. Supps said that since I had never had a behavior problem before, he would give me another chance. He said he was going to watch me, though. But it's not him I'm worried about." His voice suddenly grew lower. "Andy, she's watching us, too!" I knew he was talking about my mummy.

"I know," I whispered.

"I was going to try and explain it all to Mrs. Foley and Mr. Supps," Keg continued. "But I was afraid they'd think I was crazy or something. We've got to tell them together and show them how she works, or they'll never believe us."

"No, we can't tell them," I cried. "Not yet, anyway." I took a deep breath and waited a minute before continuing.

"Keg, this is the first time in my life that I've ever done anything special," I began. "Miss Haverly even called me gifted! Me, the loser! If we tell them about the mummy's power now, they'll all know that I didn't make her by myself. I couldn't bear to look at Jason's face when he found out. Please don't tell anyone."

"All right, I won't tell anyone for now," Keg agreed. I breathed a sigh of relief, and watched as he pulled his book from the museum out of his book bag.

"Maybe there is something in here that will help us figure things out," he said, opening the book. He turned a few pages and then began to read:

"The Egyptians believed that the *ka* was a spirit, immaterial, not like the human body. It could easily pass through walls. It could even leave the tomb temporarily and sit outside to enjoy the north wind. If the *ka* was restless or unhappy, it might leave the tomb in search of another vessel to inhabit."

"Oh, my gosh," I exclaimed. "Do you think that the *ka* belonging to the mummy in the museum was unhappy and so she left her mummy and came into me?"

"That's just what I was thinking," Keg said. "And I guess she got restless again, so she slipped into your paper mummy. Look at this picture, it looks just like the mummy we saw in the museum."

I leaned closer to get a better look.

"And look here's a message they found in her tomb." It was written in hieroglyphs, but there was a translation below it. "Five wishes for riches. But the sixth for despair," I read the words aloud. "So she did have magic powers and the ability to grant wishes."

"Wow, Andy, this is incredible," Keg whispered. "With the priestess's *ka* in your mummy, all your wishes have come true."

"Five wishes for riches. But the sixth for despair," I read the message again.

"What do you think they mean by despair?" Keg asked.

"I don't know, but I don't think it's anything too good. Let's ask Mr. Gifted. He knows everything." I leaned over into the aisle and turned around to look behind me where Jason was sitting with one of his friends. They were probably the two smartest kids in our school. They were playing a pocket game of chess, with magnetic pieces that Jason carried in his book bag.

"Hey, you guys, what's the definition of despair?" I asked.

Jason looked up from his game. "It's sadness," he said. "And a feeling of hopelessness, the way Ronald is feeling right now as he tries to save his queen." Jason turned to grin at Ronald, who screwed up his face, as he sat staring down at the tiny chessboard.

"Despair sounds pretty bad," I whispered to Keg as I turned around.

"Do you think you could die or anything?" Keg wanted to know.

"Well, dying would be really sad and hopeless, so yeah, I guess I could die." We both sat in silence as we thought about my hopelessly sad death.

"So," Keg finally said. "You'll just have to be careful and not make six wishes. How many wishes have you made so far?" he asked.

"Well, let's see," I said, closing my eyes to think. "One for Mr. Gaven to act weird and one for him to stop. That makes two. Then another one for you to act weird and another one for you to stop, that makes two more. So that would be four. I made four wishes."

"It says five wishes for riches, but the sixth for despair. Maybe by riches it means that you get what you wished for."

"I did get everything I wished for," I said.

"Yeah, that would fit. And according to this, you

72

have one more wish that will turn out good. Andy, do you know what this means?"

My eyes lit up at the thought. "It means I can wish for anything in the world! Baseball cards!" I cried.

"Bubble gum. Truckloads of bubble gum." Keg grinned.

"A monster television set in my bedroom." I sighed.

"With all the videos that have ever been made since the beginning of time," Keg added.

"They didn't make videos in the beginning of time," I pointed out.

"Okay, okay, then wish for all the videos since the beginning of video time!"

"Or pizza." I sighed. "Pepperoni pizza delivered to my house every night for a year, a whole pie, just for me."

"Or the lottery," Keg cried. "Your parents could win the lottery!

"Or AIDS!" I said. "I could wish away AIDS."

"Yeah, or cancer, or pollution, or war. You could wish for world peace." We went on and on like that for the rest of the bus ride home. There were so many things to wish for it was hard to know which wish to choose, although I knew baseball cards would have to be right up there with world peace.

Thinking of the mummy's smile was still frightening, but the thought of all that good stuff happening gave me courage. I looked out the window and saw that we had come to our stop.

"I'll see you tomorrow," I whispered to Keg. "And remember, mum's the word on the mummy." Then I grabbed my stuff and walked off the bus. Jason and I never walk with each other if we can help it. He walks with his friend Ronald, who gets off at the same stop. So I was surprised to find him running up beside me as I began walking down the sidewalk.

"I saw your mummy in the art room," he said as we walked together toward the house. "I don't know who helped you with it, but you can't fool me. You couldn't make something that good yourself."

I could feel the muscles in my face tightening. "You can ask anyone in my class," I said, trying to keep the nervousness out of my voice. "They all watched me make it." But Jason wasn't buying this. He stopped and turned to face me as we reached the front door.

"Something fishy is going on here," he said, his face growing cloudy with suspicion, "and I'm going to find out what it is." He gave me one of those looks that go right through you. A look that told me he knew how stupid I really was. As I watched him walk into the house, I clenched my fists and kicked a stone off the sidewalk.

Maybe baseball cards and world peace would have to wait. Maybe my wish shouldn't be for something to come to me, but rather for something to go away! A wide grin spread across my face as I thought of the perfect wish. I could send Jason on a long trip. In fact — I could send Jason right out of my life!

CHAPTER TEN

Once I stepped into the house, things took a turn for the better. Marie was waiting in the kitchen with cookies and milk. She was all excited, after getting a phone call from Mrs. Foley.

"Andy, I'm so proud of you," she said, putting her arms around me in a hug. "Your art teacher called to tell us about the wonderful mummy you made. She said it was the most artistically advanced piece of work that a student of hers had ever completed. I can't wait to tell your dad about it." I stole a glance at Jason, who stood frowning in the doorway. I could feel myself beginning to grin.

I spent most of that evening grinning. It was hard not to. To celebrate my amazing accomplishment, Marie made my favorite supper, baked macaroni, and Dad was so proud when he heard, that he told me I could watch an extra program on TV. Even

Winks was smiling at me more than usual. After supper, I watched her in the den while Marie and Dad finished up the dishes. I told Winks all about the mummy and I told her about my wish.

"If I send Jason away, we'll have the whole yard to ourselves," I whispered as I took off her booty and kissed her toes. She tilted her head to the side and smiled. I don't know if she was smiling because I told her about the wish or because I was kissing her toes. She loves to get her toes kissed.

"And we can take his bedroom and turn it into a really neat playroom. Maybe Dad will get you a little gym set, and we can set it up in there, and I can teach you how to work out. We could put some real muscles on you," I said, pulling on her legs. She laughed at this and I laughed, too, but stopped when I suddenly noticed Jason spying in the doorway. I put Winks's booties back on her feet in silence. Jason stood sulking as he watched. He didn't seem to be in the blue-ribbon zone anymore. I'd say he was looking a little gray around the edges, and I have to admit, I didn't mind at all.

Marie called us all back into the kitchen for dessert, and as we sat at the counter having a piece of cake, Jason began bragging again as usual.

"My dad is going to take me surfing when I go out to visit him in California, this summer," he was saying. "He lives right next door to a surf shop and he'll probably buy me my own board. He said he would take me surfing in Hawaii, when I get really good at it."

"Um, that's cool," I said, shoving a piece of chocolate cake in my mouth. Even his bragging couldn't spoil my mood. Besides, I knew that it might very well be the last bragging I'd be hearing for a long time.

"I'm going to love going to Hawaii." Jason sighed.

I'd love for you to go to Hawaii, too, I was thinking. But if you went with your dad, he would eventually send you back.

"Where else?" I asked. "Where else would you go, if you could go anywhere in the world, exploring by yourself?"

Jason sat thinking this over, as he licked a piece of icing off his cake.

"Africa," he said. "I guess I would have to say Africa, because I'd want to see the animals."

"Um, Africa, would be good," I said. Far enough away, I was thinking.

"Or out of this world," Jason suggested.

"Out of this world?" My ears pricked up.

"Yeah, space exploration, the final frontier." Jason's favorite TV show was *Star Trek*.

"Now that sounds like a great idea," I said, nodding my head.

When I finally went to my room to do my homework, it was hard to concentrate. I was wondering if I should send Jason to Mars or Jupiter. But I couldn't help thinking about all the other things I could wish for instead, like a monkey or a koala bear.

I suddenly wondered if I might be able to wish for more wishes. But as I thought it over I decided not to try. "Five wishes for riches, the sixth for despair," seemed pretty clear. I'd have to settle for sending Jason to Mars. I tried to stop thinking about all this wishing business as I started in on my homework.

Our assignment for social studies was to write a one-page report on the Nile River. I pulled a library book out of my book bag. It was all about Egypt and the Nile River. Miss Haverly had assigned us this report a week ago, and as usual I had put off doing it until the night before it was due. I usually don't like to spend too much time on homework, and most of the time I get C's on my reports, except for once when Marie helped me. That time I got a B. But as I sat paging through the library book, I wondered if I could get a B all by myself this time. Or an A. Why not an A? I had spent the whole day listening to people praise me and I suddenly decided that I didn't want it to stop.

Instead of rushing through the book and trying to get the report done as fast as I could, as I usually did, I took my time. I sat reading for a long while and found that the Nile was pretty amazing, as far as rivers go. It is the longest river in the world and without it, all of Egypt would be a desert. But the most amazing thing I found out about the Nile was that every summer the monsoons, or rains, caused the river to rise and overflow its banks. This caused the surrounding land to be flooded and the desert, which was usually beyond its reach, was left with rich deposits of earth that allowed the Egyptians to grow food and build an empire. I read and reread this sentence, "The Egyptians believed that it was the magic of the mighty Nile that transformed their lands and enriched their lives."

That sentence stuck in my mind, because with only changing a few words they could have been talking about me and my mummy.

I read it aloud again. "Andy Manetti believed that it was the magic of his mighty mummy that transformed his grades and enriched his life."

I read through most of the book, and then I began my report. I was determined to make it great. One more magnificent feat for the "Magnificent Manetti." With my colored markers, I began work on the cover. I made a picture of the Nile winding its way through the Egyptian desert, and suddenly I began having fun. I kept checking back with my book and found all kinds of things to include in the picture. I drew stalks of papyrus plants growing along the Nile, and underneath them, I wrote, "The Egyptians invented paper, using the papyrus plant." I went on to draw a little boat on the river and a towering pyramid off in the distance. I made a border of hieroglyphs around the edges of the paper. At the very bottom, just below my name, I drew a tiny mummy.

I was having so much fun working on my report, that when Dad called me to tell me my TV program was on, I told him I was too busy. By then I had finished the cover and had begun the written part. My cursive handwriting is usually so sloppy, that Miss Haverly has a hard time reading what I've written. I decided that this time it would be different, and that if I went really slowly and tried my hardest to be neat, I could write words that she'd be able to read. I looked down at my finished sentence and was amazed at how good it looked. I knew then, that this was going to be my best report yet.

I was writing the last sentence, when Dad came in to tell me it was time for bed. He looked down at my report and smiled.

"Well, I guess that little talk we had the other morning made an impression," he said as he sat down on my bed. I nodded my head. I wanted to tell him the truth, that it wasn't his little talk about the Grand Canyon, but the magic of a two-thousand-year-old mummy that was transforming my life, but I didn't. He picked up my cover page and shook his head.

"This is really great, Andy," he said. "I'm so glad

to see that you finally started caring about your schoolwork. I guess having Jason for a stepbrother has really helped."

I couldn't believe my ears. I had finally done something wonderful, so wonderful that the whole school was talking about it, and instead of patting me on the back, my own father was giving credit to Mr. Gifted! I felt my breath coming in short, angry puffs.

"Jason?" I shouted, throwing down my pen. "I'm sick of him. I wish he never moved here. He didn't have anything to do with my mummy, and he's got nothing to do with me. Why doesn't he go back and live with his father, then we'd all be happy." I glared down at my report, not wanting to look at my dad, but I could hear him sigh.

"I'm sorry you feel that way," he said. His voice was low and sad. "But there are some people who I think you've forgotten about here. Marie, for one. Jason is Marie's son. Do you think she would feel happy if Jason were to move away? Jason's dad moved all the way to California, and if Jason were to live with him again, Marie wouldn't be able to see him."

I sat staring down at my pillow.

"And then there's Jason to think of," Dad continued. "Don't you think he wants a chance to be with his mother?" The words stung as I fought back the tears.

"What about me?" I said. "Don't you think I'd like a chance to be with *my* mother?" Dad was so startled that he threw back his head, as if I had hit him.

"What are you talking about?" he shot back.

"My mother," I said, feeling the tears in my eyes. "I had one, too, remember? And you never mention her. Don't you think I'd like a chance to be with her? I know I can't see her or touch her, but don't you think I'd like to hear about her? You're so worried about somebody else's son, what about your own? Aren't I important, too?"

I hadn't meant to say all of that. It just came pouring out, and I couldn't stop myself. Dad sat for a long time staring down at the bed and not saying anything. He looked as if he were about to cry, when he suddenly stood up and walked out the door. I sunk back on my pillow and closed my eyes.

Why did it have to be like this? I wondered. Why did I have to have a mother who died and a stepbrother like Jason? Why couldn't my dad understand, and why couldn't he be proud of the things I did, without Jason getting the credit?

I thought about how I wished my life were different as I sat up and stared down at the little mummy on my cover page. That's when I thought of my mummy at school, and thought about wishing for something really big, not baseball cards, or monkeys, or even sending Mr. Gifted to Mars.

I felt a shiver of excitement as I sat thinking about

it. It was so simple, I wondered why I hadn't thought of it before. I could wish for something that would not only get rid of Jason, but something that would change my life forever, a wish that would solve all my problems. My mother! I could wish for my mother.

After tomorrow, my life would really be transformed. I could just see myself walking into Miss Haverly's classroom and taking my seat. I would stare up at my mummy, and looking into those deep-blue eyes, I would wish with all my might that my mother had never died.

CHAPTER ELEVEN

I woke up the next morning and the first thing I thought of was my mother. What would she be like? Would she look like me? Would she sound like me? Would she like me? A thousand questions went through my mind, as I searched for my good shirt in my drawer. I wanted to look my best, because I knew that after I made my wish, I would come home from school and find her waiting for me. How would I get through a whole day of school, knowing that she would be here?

I ran into the bathroom and brushed my teeth about a hundred times, because I knew that mothers liked their kids to have clean teeth. I would have brushed them more, if Jason hadn't begun to whine that I was hogging the sink. Then he began to whine that I was using too much toothpaste, and that the towel was wet. He wasn't usually this grouchy in the morning, and I wondered what his problem was.

Well, I thought to myself, as I walked out into the hall, you can be as grouchy as you want to be, because it's going to be the last time you'll be using my bathroom and my toothpaste and my towel. And you're lucky that I didn't send you to Mars. I doubt that they would have bathrooms on Mars.

I walked into the kitchen, and Marie smiled at me. A big, warm smile. I wished she wouldn't do that.

"How are you feeling?" she asked.

"Okay, I guess," I told her. I thought she was talking about my talk with Dad last night. I felt embarrassed about what I had said. I didn't want to hurt Marie's feelings.

"Well, Jason's got a sore throat and a temperature," Marie was saying. "He's staying home from school today. Are you sure you feel all right? If you don't feel good, you can stay home, too."

"No!" I cried. "I feel fine, really." Usually I would have jumped at the chance to stay home, but not today.

"I wonder if your dad is coming down with something. He was so quiet last night," Marie said, looking out the window.

I knew then he didn't tell her about our fight, and I suddenly felt bad about having to wish Marie away. I really liked having her around.

I sat down at the table and poured some cereal into my bowl. Dad walked into the kitchen carrying Winks, and placed her in her baby swing by the table. Dad wouldn't look at me, and I wouldn't look at him. This is what we do whenever we have a fight. It usually takes a day or two for us to start talking again.

As I began to eat my cereal in silence, I thought about how glad Dad would be to see my mom waiting for him after work today. I know he cares for Marie, but it couldn't be the same as the way he felt for my mom. And if I wished for my mom never to have died, then he wouldn't have ever met Marie. So he couldn't miss her. I tried to imagine him and my mom together. She looked really pretty in the picture I have of her.

I was trying to imagine my mother standing at the sink, when I heard Jason's whiny voice. I looked up to see him coming toward the table. He had gotten out of his pajamas and was dressed for school.

"I'm not staying home," he was saying.

"I'm sorry, but you cannot go to school with a temperature and a sore throat," Marie told him.

"I have to," Jason screeched. "I don't want to miss the spelling bee." Jason always does great in spelling bees.

"But, Jason," Marie pleaded. "You're sick, honey, and they won't even let you in school with a temperature."

"I don't care," Jason snapped. "I'm going. You can't stop me."

"Hold on, right there, bud," Dad said, raising his voice. "If your mother says you're going to stay home, then that's where you're staying."

"You can't tell me what to do," Jason suddenly shouted. "You're not my father." I shot a look at Dad. His face was turning red.

"Let's get something straight, right now," Dad shouted back. My dad's voice is deep, and when he shouts he sounds like a bear. I had never heard him use his bear shout on Jason before. "While you're living under my roof," he went on, "you'll do as you're told. Now get yourself back in your bed, before you make me do something we'll both be sorry for." I couldn't believe my ears, he was actually yelling at Jason. And I couldn't believe Jason was stupid enough to answer back.

"I'm not afraid of you," Jason yelled. "You can't make me do anything I don't want to."

"That's it!" Dad bellowed, pushing himself back from the table as he stood up. "You've gone too far this time. You're acting like a spoiled brat, and you're going to stop it right now."

Winks began to cry at this outburst, and Marie went to pick her up, while Jason dashed for his room with Dad stomping behind him. I sat at the table stunned. I never dreamed I'd see the day when Dad would yell like that at Mr. Gifted. Winks was still crying, and Marie looked as if she were about to cry herself.

"Andy," she whispered anxiously. "Go and get your sneakers on, or you'll miss your bus." I went to my room, and was tying up my laces when I heard Marie's voice coming from the kitchen.

"Phil, I don't believe you blew up at him that way. You know he's not feeling well."

Then I heard Dad shouting. "What am I supposed to do? Let him talk to me like that? Let him do just as he pleases? He's ten years old, Marie. I'm the adult. I keep the roof over his head. I'm feeding him and keeping him in those fancy sneakers. Is that the thanks I get? I didn't run out on the kid, like his father did. I didn't go traipsing off to California to 'find myself.' I'm out there laying block all day, so he can have a nice place to live, so you all can."

"I know, I know," Marie was saying.

"No, you don't know. You don't!" Dad's voice sounded mad and sad at the same time. I heard the kitchen door slam, and Winks began to cry all over again. After a little while, I heard the clicking of her swing, and she quieted down. I waited and then walked back into the kitchen to get my lunch.

"Can you make yourself a sandwich?" Marie said

weakly. We could both hear Jason crying in his room.

"Sure," I mumbled.

"Keep an eye on the baby," she said. "I'll be right back."

I made myself a peanut-butter-and-jelly sandwich, and knelt down by the swing. I offered Winks my finger to lick. She seemed to like strawberry jelly. Then I picked up her toy pig from the floor and placed it in her hands. As I knelt down beside her, I could hear Jason and Marie from the bedroom.

"Why did he have to go to California?" Jason was asking between sobs. "Why couldn't he have taken me with him? Why doesn't he love me the way Phil loves Andy?"

I was so startled to hear this that I didn't even hear what Marie was answering. It suddenly occurred to me that Jason thought his father didn't love him. Since he's been here, I've felt nothing but envy for Jason and all his blue ribbons, but for the first time I was feeling something else. I felt sorry for him. I tried to imagine how I would feel if my dad ran off to California. I knew about losing a parent, but my mom didn't run off. She died, and that's different. Maybe if Marie hadn't met Dad, I thought, she wouldn't have left Jason's dad and he wouldn't have left for California.

When Marie came back into the kitchen, I went

to my room to get my book bag. As I passed Jason's door, I could hear him crying. I tried to keep walking on past, but I couldn't. He sounded so sad. And I knew it might be the last time I would ever see him again. My hand tightened around his doorknob before I had the nerve to turn it. I coughed a couple of times, and he stopped crying. I walked into his room and stood by the dresser. He was sitting on his bed, twisting the end of his sheet in his hand.

"What do you want?" he asked, wiping his eyes on his pajama shirt.

"I just wondered if you wanted me to get your homework assignments, so you won't miss anything today," I told him. Jason's red ringed eyes met mine.

"Since when do you care?"

"I don't know," I muttered. "I . . . I . . ."

"You what?" he demanded. "You and your dad couldn't care less about me. You've both hated me since the first day I came here. And Mom is so busy with the baby that she never has time for me. No one cares about me."

I stood squirming, not knowing what to say. It was true, I had hated him, but I knew Dad didn't.

"My dad is always comparing me to you," I told him. "But I don't think he hates you as much as I do."

Jason shrugged. "I just wish my dad were here right now," he whimpered, pulling the pillowcase

91

off of his pillow. He sniffled a bit and then began to pull a feather out of a tiny hole in the corner of his pillow. I never realized that Jason pulled out his pillow feathers the same way I did.

"I know how you feel," I told him, sitting on the edge of his bed. I held my breath, waiting to see if he would push me off. He didn't.

"How could you know?" he snapped. "You have a dad who lives with you, a dad who cares about you."

"I was talking about my mom," I tried to explain. "I've wished for my mom the way you've wished for your dad." I bit down on my lip. "I always thought we were so different, you and me," I said. "But I guess we have the same kind of problem."

I wanted to tell him that I was sorry about hating him and that, if he could just stop bragging all the time, people might like him more, at least I might. I wanted to tell him how I had always dreamed about having a brother who I could be best friends with, and how disappointed I was that we hadn't hit it off.

Then I suddenly found myself wondering if he had ever wanted the same thing. I guessed he did and I supposed he must be just as disappointed in me as I was in him. I wanted to ask him about it, but somehow I couldn't get the words out. I sat watching as he pulled another feather from his pillow.

"That's a good one," I said. He nodded his head and handed it to me. I stood up and started for the door, when I heard him say, "See ya later."

My fist tightened around the tiny feather.

"Yeah," I struggled to say, pulling the door shut behind me. But no, is what I wanted to yell. No, you won't see me later, because you'll be gone.

I walked out of the room, and stood for a minute in the hall. Leaning against Jason's closed door, I opened my fist.

"I'm sorry," I whispered, looking down at the curled white feather in my palm. "But if I don't wish for my mother now, I'll never get another chance."

"Andy, quick, the bus is coming!" Marie yelled. I took off down the hall, never even feeling the feather fall from my fingers.

CHAPTER TWELVE

"So what's it going to be?" Keg asked. "Truckloads of pizza or a bubble gum factory?"

"I'm going to wish for my mom," I whispered.

"You're going to wish for what?" Keg cried, on hearing me.

"My mom," I said softly. "I'm going to wish that my mom had never died."

"What a great wish!" Keg sighed. "It's even better than a bubble gum factory. But what's wrong? Why aren't you happier looking?" That's when I explained to him about Jason and I watched the look of horror come over his face.

"Wish away your stepbrother?" he whispered. "I don't know, Andy. I've thought about wishing away my sisters a lot, but I don't know if I could ever go through with it."

"It's not that I'm wishing him away, it's just that it's the only way I can have my mother," I told him.

I went on to explain about my fight with Dad and Jason's feeling bad and Marie's feeling bad. "It's the worst," I told him.

Keg understood. "Sometimes it gets like that in our house, too, and nobody has even died or run off to California."

"How do you stand it?" I asked.

"Oh, I don't know." He shrugged. "It doesn't last too long. Everyone yells and then they make up and feel good again until someone starts yelling again."

I thought about this and about my situation. I didn't see how I could feel good again, knowing that I had a chance to be with my mom and didn't take it. By the time the bus pulled up to school, my stomach was in knots.

"Andy," Keg turned to me, putting his hand on my shoulder. "I know how you feel, and it must be hard, but could we talk about another wish for a minute?"

"What other wish?"

"Well," Keg said, hesitating. "A wish for Wiley."

"You want me to wish that Wiley was alive?"

"No, no," Keg said. "Megan already has a new hamster, Dustball, and there's only room in the cage for one. No, I've already got Wiley's tomb made and everything. It's just that every time I think about actually doing it, you know, mummifying him, I get the creeps. I was just wondering if maybe you could wish him into a mummy for me."

"You want me to wish for some old dead hamster to be mummified, instead of wishing for my mother to come alive?" I cried.

"Well, no, you don't have to put it like that," Keg said, squirming in his seat. "I was just thinking if you decided not to wish for your mom, because of Jason and Marie and all, and you didn't know what else to wish for. It would really help me out, and I am your best friend."

I spent the rest of the bus ride thinking about my mother and Wiley's mummy. When we got to Miss Haverly's class, the first thing I noticed was my mummy hanging back up on the bulletin board. I quickly looked away, for the gaze of those eyes seemed to go right through me.

"I hear your mummy spent the afternoon in the art room," Miss Haverly was saying as I walked to my desk. "Mrs. Foley brought it back this morning. And I have good news for you, Andy. She's selected it as one of the school's entries in the Barton Museum's Children's Gallery. You should be quite proud of yourself. Just think, your artwork will be hanging in a museum!"

"That's great," I mumbled, trying not to look at the bulletin board.

"The school has till the end of the week to finish making their selections," Miss Haverly continued. "Then all the artwork will be taken to the museum and all participants will be invited to come with their friends and families to an opening on Saturday."

"An opening?" I asked.

"Yes, that's when they open a new show at a gallery or museum. It's like a party to celebrate the new work."

"Will there be food?" Keg wanted to know.

"Yes, Keggan, they usually have little fancy sandwiches, or cookies and punch. So if you're interested you'd better hurry and finish your project. There are only a few days left before the rest of the selections are made." Keg gave me a knowing look.

"I love those little fancy sandwiches," he mumbled. I opened my desk and looked inside. I wasn't looking for anything, I just didn't want to have to look in the direction of my mummy, but when Mrs. Foley walked into the room, I was forced to look up.

"Oh, Andrew, have you heard the good news?" she asked brightly as she stood before the bulletin board.

"Yes, I was just telling him all about it," Miss Haverly said.

"So you won't mind if we borrow your mummy for a while, will you?" she asked.

"You want to hang her back up in the art room?" I asked.

"No," Mrs. Foley replied. "We're going to bring it to the museum to use for advertising the upcoming opening of the Children's Gallery."

"When?" Keg spoke up. "When would you take the mummy?"

"Today," Mrs. Foley said. "After my morning classes, I'll be going to the museum to meet with the director. I'd like to take it with me then." She turned and stared up at my mummy. "Magnificent, just magnificent." She sighed before walking to the door. Miss Haverly followed her out into the hall, where the two stood talking. Keg turned around in his seat and tapped on my desktop. I had raised it so I could stick my head all the way in.

"What are you hiding in there for?" he whispered. "Didn't you hear what Mrs. Foley said? Your mummy is going to the museum today!"

"So?"

"Don't you remember what we were reading on the bus, about the *ka* leaving the tomb and then sometimes returning? When Mrs. Foley brings your mummy back to the museum, the priestess's *ka* might return to its original mummy. This morning may be the only time you have to make your wish. You'd better do it now, or you may never get the chance again."

I bit down on my lip. I knew he was right. I thought of my mother. When would I ever get a chance to make such a wish? The room suddenly grew noisy as kids began rushing to take their seats.

"Go on," Keg coaxed. "Do it now."

I jumped at the sudden sound of the bell. In a haze I saw Miss Haverly standing in front of her desk. She was saying something, but I couldn't hear her over the sound of my heart pounding in my ears.

"Now," Keg insisted, turning around in his seat. "Now!"

My throat suddenly became dry, as I realized I was about to call on the ancient powers of the priestess. A priestess who had lived and died over two thousand years ago! I now knew that with this wish, I would be reaching back in time, to summon the magic and mysteries of ancient Egypt. A thin little breeze tickled the back of my neck as I raised my eyes to meet the cold gaze of the mummy's eyes.

CHAPTER THIRTEEN

"After I take attendance," Miss Haverly was saying, "we'll be getting right to your reports on the Nile, so please get them out. I'll be choosing three people to read their reports in front of the class." The sound of papers rustling suddenly filled the room. I opened my social studies folder and took out my report.

"Have you done it yet?" Keg asked, turning around.

"I'll do it, I'll do it," I said. "I just need a little more time."

"You only have a little time," he reminded me.

I knew Keg was right, but he wasn't the one having to wish away his stepmother and stepbrother. I thought about Marie and her smiling face. Then I thought of Jason and his constant bragging, and his crying about his dad moving away to California.

I thought about the sad look on my dad's face when I mentioned my mom. I imagined the look on his face when my wish came true and he got to see her again. I imagined him laughing and she'd be laughing, too. We'd all be laughing and hugging and just so happy to be together at last. I took a deep breath and looked back up at my mummy. I was all ready to do it, when I heard someone calling my name.

At first I thought it might be my mother, but then I remembered I hadn't made the wish yet. I looked down from my mummy to see Miss Haverly staring at me.

"Andy, didn't you hear me?" she was saying.

"Huh?"

"I asked if you would please come up to the front of the room and read us your report on the Nile," Miss Haverly said. I looked over at Keg, who was rolling his eyes, and then I picked up my report and walked to the front of the room. I looked at my mummy, and then quickly down at my report.

Usually, when I have to read in front of the class, I'm so nervous that the words get all jumbled up, and I sound really stupid, but I was so preoccupied with thinking about my wish that I didn't think to be nervous. I began reading, and the words just flowed out like they were supposed to. After the first paragraph, I even started to enjoy myself. Since

I had spent so much time on my report, it was fun to read it aloud. I was actually proud of what I had done. Miss Haverly was proud, too.

"Congratulations, Andy," she said when I was through and had handed her my paper. "That was a wonderful report." She looked down at my paper. "Your penmanship has really improved. You must have put a lot of effort into this."

I shook my head and grinned as I walked back to my seat. Another magnificent moment. Miss Haverly called Max Silvestri up next. Max was one of the smartest kids in our class. He always got A's on his reports.

"Good going, Andy," Max said as he passed my desk. I couldn't stop smiling and, as I began to listen to Max's report, I realized that mine had been just as good as his!

After a while, my eyes began to wander over to the clock above the door, and my smile began to fade. I knew it wasn't long before the morning would be over, and Mrs. Foley would be ready to go to the musuem. I sat staring at the minute hand, watching as it slowly crawled around the clock's face. And with each revolution of the hand, I knew I was that much closer to losing all chances of making my wish. If I was going to do it, it would have to be now. I turned to face my mummy. I felt a chill sweep down my spine. She seemed to be looking directly at me!

As we locked gazes, I thought of all the magnificent things that had happened in the last few days. Ever since you came, I was thinking, my life has gotten better and better, and now I wish . . . I wish . . . I wish my mother could be with me, forever and ever.

CHAPTER FOURTEEN

"That's funny," Mrs. Foley was saying later that day as Keg and I carried my mummy into the art room. "Somehow I remember your mummy as having a different expression on her face. Was she always smiling that way?"

Keg and I looked down nervously at my mummy's mysterious grin, and our hands began to tremble, causing the paper to shake.

"Oh, boys, please don't fool around like that," Mrs. Foley scolded, forgetting all about the smile as she took the mummy from us. "This is a very important piece of art, and it must be handled with care." She began gently rolling the mummy around a long cylinder of cardboard. As I stood watching, I felt a wave of relief wash over me. My mummy was going! Going back to the priestess and the power that created her. I felt as if a weight were off my chest. It was no longer up to me to wish for the right thing.

And what about the wish I had made? What would it be like going home to my real mother? I spent the rest of the day looking up at the clock and biting my nails. How was I going to last until three? I was almost glad to find that we were having a surprise quiz in math, at least I could think about something else for a while.

I looked up to the front of the room, to see Mr. Gaven (with his hair sitting on the middle of his head where it belonged) handing out the quiz papers. He was smiling smugly, obviously enjoying the look of pain on our faces, as we sat sweaty palmed, expecting the worst. I quickly looked over the problems, and I could tell it was going to be bad. There were such long problems, I didn't see how I would ever finish. But this was how I usually felt when I took a test or quiz. That same overwhelming feeling of failure would come over me, and it was as if my brain would suddenly slow up.

I looked up to see Mr. Gaven, still smiling. "All right, people, you'd better get started if you hope to finish," he said. I hated the sound of his voice. It was almost as if he hoped we wouldn't finish, as if he were daring us.

I'll show you who's going to finish, I was thinking, as I began to tackle the first problem. And then it became almost like a game. I couldn't wait to finish one problem so I could go on to the next. My brain was suddenly working faster than it had ever worked.

When I finally raised my head after finishing the last problem, I could see that Max and the other smart kids had already handed in their papers. They always finished first, so I wasn't surprised. But what did surprise me was the number of kids still working! I always finish last, and a lot of the time I don't even finish at all. But today was different, because not only did I finish, but I wasn't last!

The best surprise of all came when Mr. Gaven had us exchange papers to correct our quizzes. When I got my paper back, I found out that I didn't fail, or get a D. I didn't even get a C! I got a B−!

Thank you, Miss Mummy, I was thinking, as I turned to look at the bulletin board. She wasn't there, of course, since Mrs. Foley had taken her to the museum, and that's when I realized that it was possible that my mummy may have had nothing to do with this quiz. Had I gotten the B− all by myself?

"Pass the papers forward before you leave, people," I heard Mr. Gaven command. I passed my paper to Keg, whose eyebrows shot up when he saw the B− on it. We went back to the coat closet to get our jackets.

"Hey, Andy, do you want to come over my house

to play later?" Max Silvestri asked as he came up beside me. I couldn't believe that the smartest kid in our class was asking me to his house. I started to say yes, when I felt a jab in my side. It was Keg.

"Are you crazy?" he whispered. "You can't go today. We've got to check out your wish. To see if you got it."

My wish! Of course! What was I thinking of? I quickly mumbled some excuse to Max and promised to go over to his house another day.

"Aren't you excited?" Keg was asking later, as we sat on the bus. "I don't know how you could make such a great wish and not even look excited!"

I closed my eyes. I was excited. Too excited for words. As I put my head back on the bus seat, I squeezed my eyes shut tighter. I imagined my mom giving me a big hug when I walked into the house. I imagined her arms around me, but when I looked up to her face it was cloudy and I couldn't make out her features.

"Hey, Manetti, it's your stop," Devin Ritter, the bus guard, yelled.

"I'll call you as soon as I get home and we can talk all about it," Keg called after me as I dragged myself along the aisle, toward the front of the bus. I made my way down the steps and onto the sidewalk. As I headed toward my house, my steps grew smaller and smaller. I inched my way along, as if in slow motion. As much as I wanted to see my mother, I was suddenly afraid. What would she be like? Would she recognize me?

Finally after what seemed like hours, I reached my house. I looked through the picture window into the living room, but no one seemed to be inside. I turned my head and searched the yard, expecting to see them, Dad and my mom and Winks. And that's when it hit me.

"Winks! Oh my gosh, no," I gasped. If my wish had come true, I would have wished away Marie, and she would have never met Dad — and they would have never had Winks. How could I be so stupid? By wishing for my mother, I had wished my baby sister right out of existence!

CHAPTER FIFTEEN

"Andy, Andy. Come on in here. Someone has been waiting for you to come home all afternoon." It was my dad calling, as he stuck his head out of the garage door, and I suddenly knew who he was talking about. I tried to look inside the garage, but it was too dark to see from where I was standing. My knees suddenly felt wobbly and my hands were sweaty.

A few more steps, I was thinking. All I have to do is take a few more steps and I'll be face to face with the person I've always wanted to meet for as long as I can remember. My mother! I was about to meet my mother! But the shock of it left me unable to move, that and the shock of losing Winks. It was as if the very best thing that could ever happen in my life was happening along with the very worst thing. I felt like laughing and crying at the same time.

"Don't just stand there, come on in," Dad said

as he walked over to me and grabbed my arm. "But first close your eyes." I closed my eyes and let him lead me into the garage. My heart felt as if it were going to leap out of my chest with each step. Why didn't she say something? Why didn't she talk? Where was she standing? I wondered, as I stood waiting in the cold silence of the garage. My ears were like antennae, roaming around in the dark, trying to pick up any sound. I did hear something that sounded like a little gurgle.

"Okay, now," Dad said. I could hear the excitement in his voice. "Go ahead and open your eyes."

I was so scared, I didn't know if I could move a muscle. It took all my courage, but I was finally able to crack open one eye. I first looked out the garage window into the backyard, and when I did, I was so shocked, I nearly fell over backward.

"Oh, no!" I gasped, for the sight that met my eyes sent a shudder through me. It was our yard, all right. My hideout was there, and so was the clothesline, and the big old oak tree, but something was missing. I felt my heart breaking, as I stood looking at the long empty branch of the oak tree. A branch that had once held a small red swing. I blinked several times, hoping that I had made a mistake, hoping to see that tiny wooden swing. But it was gone, vanished, as if it had never been there!

"Oh, no, Winks," I whimpered as a tear rolled down my cheek. "I'm so sorry. I'm so sorry."

Dad turned me around and led me to the other side of the garage, and my heart pounded as my eyes adjusted to the dim light. And then, my heart swelled with happiness at what I saw.

"Winks!" I cried. "It's you! It's really you!" For swinging before me was Winks! Her little red swing that had hung from the tree was now hanging from an old rusty swing frame. She blinked on hearing my voice and then smiled. I stood staring now, with both eyes opened wide, as I tried to figure out what was going on.

"Well, of course, it's really her," Dad was saying as he adjusted the strap around Winks's waist. "Who else could fit in that little swing? So how do you like it?" he asked, turning to look at me.

"Like it?" I mumbled. I was having a hard time taking everything in. Winks was here, and so that must mean my mother wasn't. I was relieved and yet disappointed at the same time. My wish hadn't come true. My mother wasn't there.

"Her new swing set," Dad was saying, "I got it on a job. This guy was going to put it out for the garbage men. All it really needed was a new seat, so I took down her swing from the yard. That old oak is going to need pruning soon. This will be safer, too. Of course we'll need to paint it, and since you're the family artist, I thought you could give me a hand."

"The family artist?" I mumbled.

"Manetti, the Magnificent Mummy Maker, isn't that what everyone is calling you at school?"

"Yeah, I guess so, but how did you know?" I said.

"Jason told Marie. I think he was a little jealous, to tell you the truth." Dad grinned sheepishly. "I wasn't surprised to hear it though."

"You weren't?"

"No, because I figured you must have inherited all that artistic stuff."

My dad is good at a lot of things but I had never known that he was good in art. "From you?" I asked.

"Not from me, from your mother," Dad said softly. "Annie was always drawing and painting. She was a very good artist."

"Annie." I shivered at the sound of it. It was the first time I had ever heard him say her name. I lowered my eyes. I don't know why, but I was suddenly embarrassed.

"Andy," Dad said. I knew he was waiting for me to look up at him. When I finally did there were tears in his eyes and his voice was low and quavery. "I know I haven't done right by you," he said, "by not talking about your mother and all. I thought it would be better to wait until you were older, but I guess I was just trying to put it off because it was so hard to talk about. She was such a special person. It's still hard, you know, even after all these years . . ." His voice trailed off into a sob as he lowered his head.

"It's okay, Dad," I whispered. "You don't have to talk about her if you don't want to." I had never seen him cry before, and it scared me.

"No," he said, wiping his eyes and lifting his head to look at me. "A little at a time, we'll go a little at a time. She was so much like you, Andy. Sometimes I feel her presence so strongly in you, the way you tilt your head to the side when you laugh, or the way you're so good with your sister. Your mother always loved babies, too. And now with your artistic talent, why it's as if she's returned somehow." He shook his head and tried to smile. "So Mr. Magnificent, since you now know where all that artistic stuff comes from, do you think you could put some of it to use and help me with your sister's swing set?"

"Sure," I grinned, looking over at Winks.

"Marie," he called. "Can you come and get the baby? Andy and I have some work to do."

"Hi, Andy," Marie said when she walked into the garage. "How are you feeling? You didn't come down with Jason's bug, did you?"

"No, I'm fine."

"And what do you think of the swing set?" she wanted to know.

"It's great," I told her. "It's really great."

"It's still going to need some work," Dad said. And as I watched him lift Winks out of the swing and put her into Marie's arms, I knew that I really did feel fine, and I was glad things had worked out the way they had. My mother had died long ago and I never really knew her. But I've known Winks since she was born. And I love her more than anything.

"Andy," Jason called from the kitchen. "Keg's on the phone." I stood watching Marie, Dad, and Winks for a minute longer. It felt so good to see them all together.

"Andy," Marie finally said. "Didn't you hear Jason calling? You have a phone call." I nodded my head and went on into the house where I found Jason sitting at the kitchen counter.

"It's Keggan and he says it's urgent," Jason said, in his smirkiest voice. "Do you need me to tell you the definition for 'urgent'?"

Mars, I thought to myself as I picked up the phone. Why didn't I wish for Mars?

"Andy, what's Jason still doing there? Didn't your wish come true?" Keg asked.

"Yeah," I answered. "In a way. But things worked out a little differently than I thought they would."

"So Jason stayed, but what about your mom? Did she come back, or not?" Keg whispered.

"Yeah, she came back," I said.

"Wow! So what's she like?" Keg asked excitedly.

I thought for a minute and then smiled. "She's a lot like me."

CHAPTER SIXTEEN

After Keg called, I rode my bike over to his house and once we were in his bedroom, I told him about everything that had happened. He was disappointed that my mom wasn't actually there in the flesh, but when I told him about Winks and how I had almost wished her out of existence, he agreed with me that things had worked out pretty good.

"So how did it go with Wiley?" I asked, sitting down on his bed.

"Look under the pillow," he said.

I leaned over and slowly lifted the pillow, to find a perfect little mummy, wrapped in white linen bandages. There was even a slight perfume in the air around him. I sniffed. It smelled like vanilla.

"When you told me that you were going to wish for your mother, I knew I would have to work on Wiley myself, but I couldn't do the embalming part, it was just too creepy, so I decided to make him a temporary mummy."

"A temporary mummy?"

"Yeah, you know, the kind that doesn't last for two thousand years. The kind you bury after a week or so."

"So, what exactly *did* you do to him?" I asked, staring down at the miniature mummy.

"Well, not too much really," Keg admitted. "I wrapped him in the bandages I found in our medicine cabinet and then I poured a bottle of vanilla extract over him."

"Vanilla extract?"

"Yeah," Keg grinned. "My mom was making cupcakes, and I saw the bottle on the counter and took a sniff. It's got a good smell, don't you think?" I nodded my head in agreement.

"After I poured on the vanilla extract," Keg continued. "The bandages turned brown, so I had to wrap him again and again and again!" Keg laughed. "So what do you think, isn't he a beauty?"

I don't know that I'd call him a beauty, but I had to admit that Wiley was looking very Egyptian.

"I can't wait to take him to school tomorrow and put him in his tomb. I wonder how his *ka* will like it."

As I stood staring down at the little Wiley mummy, I wondered how my paper mummy was doing now that it was back in the museum. Had the priestess's *ka* returned to her mummy? Was it finally happy? I hoped so, because I knew that we'd be going to the museum on Saturday for the opening, and I'd had my fill of powerful priestesses and mummies and wishes.

Later that afternoon, I was still thinking about mummies as I sat on my bed doing my homework. I had almost completed a page of math problems, and it had taken me a long time. I stared down at the page full of neatly penciled numbers. In the past I would have rushed through the work as fast as I could, and I would have gotten quite a few wrong. But ever since I had made my mummy, I found myself trying harder when it came to schoolwork.

There was only one more problem to go, but try as I might, I couldn't figure it out. I knew that I needed help. I would have asked Dad, but he says that math is like a foreign language to him, and Marie is no better at it. There was only one person in our house that could figure this problem out.

In the past I would have died before I asked Jason for any help, but I was beginning to feel differently about him. Oh, sure, he was still his obnoxious Mr. Gifted self, but he was also someone like me in a way. He was missing his dad, the way I had often missed my mother.

I knocked on Jason's door.

"Enter," he commanded. (Jason never said

"come in" like normal people.) He was sitting on his bed reading the dictionary, probably for fun, and when he looked up to see me, there was a look of surprise on his face. I walked over to his bed and sat down.

"I was wondering if you could help me with a math problem?" I said, holding up my paper.

"I thought you were going to get extra help in school?" he said.

"I was," I told him, "but Miss Haverly has some kind of teacher workshop all this week, and the substitute teacher we have is really mean."

"Mr. Gaven?" Jason cracked a smile.

"Yeah." I nodded. "Do you know him?"

"We have him this week, too, for our morning math class. I think if he ever tried to smile, his whole body would go into shock. We call him *"Krabbe des Yahres."*

"What does that mean?" I asked.

"It's German for 'Crab of the Year.' It kind of fits, doesn't it?"

"Crab of the Year, yeah, that does fit." I laughed. "Say it again in German, so I can tell Keg." Jason taught me that along with the German words for mush muscles, toad breath, and fur ball. I never realized that learning a foreign language could be so interesting.

I didn't mention my mummy, but I did tell him all about Mr. Gaven's sliding hair. We laughed so hard, we almost fell off the bed. It's a strange thing to be laughing with someone you never liked. It's as if, for that moment, you're both friends, even if you don't want to be, and when you're through, you somehow find yourself liking that person a little bit more. I don't know that I'll ever like Jason a lot, but laughing with him that night I didn't think I could ever hate him again, the way I once did.

"So, tell me," he asked as I stood up to leave. "How did you really make that mummy?"

"I had help," I confessed.

"I knew it!" he cried, jumping up on his bed. "Who? Who helped you?"

"Ancient Egypt," I told him. "I had a little help from ancient Egypt." On hearing this Jason sank back down to his knees.

"I'm still going to find out," he said, shaking his head.

"I don't know, this might be one even Mr. Gifted won't be able to figure out." I shot him a grin before walking out the door.

"Don't count on it, Mr. Magnificent," he called after me.

"Mr. Magnificent." I could get used to the sound of that. Later, as I was helping Dad paint the new swing set, I found myself thinking about all the magnificent things that had happened to me since I first made my mummy. I hadn't been shot down at the chalkboard, I had written the best report of my life, and I had even gotten a B− on a math quiz. But now that the mummy was gone, I wondered if I could still do magnificent things on my own.

"Dad, do you have any other colors?" I asked, after dipping my brush into the blue paint.

"Sure, I've got a bunch of old cans." Dad said, walking over to a collection of paint cans on a shelf. "That's a good idea. We can do better than ordinary old blue."

"Much better." I grinned as he handed me a can of red paint. By the time we were through we had painted the swing a whole rainbow of colors. That's what Marie called it anyway.

"It's wonderful!" she cried when she and Winks came out to look. "Just like a rainbow."

"It was Andy's idea," Dad told her. And as we all stood admiring the bright red stripes and orange and green swirls, I couldn't help but wonder how I had ever thought of myself as gray! Gray was such an ordinary color. I was feeling much more than that. I was feeling like I had a whole rainbow of colors inside of me.

CHAPTER SEVENTEEN

Wiley, the mummy, was almost as big a success as my paper mummy. At school, the next day, all the kids gathered around the little cardboard pyramid, to peek inside at the perfectly wrapped miniature mummy, lying in a coffin that had once been a Cracker Jacks box. Bits of the Cracker Jacks were lovingly laid out, along with the prize that had been at the bottom of the box. It was still in its paper wrapper. Keg felt that by not opening the prize, he was making a supreme gesture of respect. He wanted Wiley's *ka* to be able to enjoy the thrill of opening it himself. There were also some pieces of lettuce and an old hamster wheel that had once been a favorite of Wiley's. All this attention to detail did not go unnoticed.

At the end of the week, when Mrs. Foley read off the names of the students whose projects had been selected for the Barton Museum's Children's Gallery, Keg's was on it as well as mine. Jason's was on it, too, and I was surprised to find myself actually feeling glad for him.

On Saturday morning, our entire family piled into the station wagon to make the trip to the museum. Winks sat in her car seat between Jason and me. We spent most of the trip trying to get her to wink, but she wouldn't. The best we could get out of her was a blink.

"Maybe we should call her Blinks," Jason suggested. We had some fun trying to think of new nicknames for her, but decided that she was more of a Winks than anything. Even Marie had begun to call her that.

"Here we are," Dad suddenly said as we pulled into the museum's parking lot. I had been having so much fun with Jason and Winks in the car that I had forgotten where we were going and, now that we were there, I couldn't wait to go inside. I was still a little afraid of my mummy, but not as much as before, and I was anxious to see what had happened to the priestess's *ka*. I hoped it would be as happy as I was.

Jason and I led the way up the marble steps and through the museum's big glass doors. Then we followed the arrows to a big brightly lit room filled with displays of kids' art. A long pink banner, with the words CHILDREN'S GALLERY, hung from the ceiling.

"Andy!" Mrs. Foley cried when she saw me. "And these must be your parents, Mr. and Mrs. Manetti." She reached for Dad's hand to shake, and then Marie's. "You have two very talented boys," she was saying as I nervously looked around. That's when I saw Keg. He was walking toward me with his parents and three sisters. Soon everyone was shaking hands and talking excitedly and, in all the commotion, Keg and I were able to slip away.

"There she is," Keg whispered. "Down there." We made our way through the crowd of parents and kids, until we were finally standing before my paper mummy. Her cold blue eyes stared down at us. Keg was fidgeting nervously beside me.

"She's not smiling anymore," he whispered. I stood staring at my mummy for a long while.

"She's not smiling because she's only paper," I finally mumbled.

"What do you mean?"

"The priestess's *ka* has left her," I told him.

"How do you know?"

"It's her eyes," I said. "They're different, somehow. It's hard to explain, but she doesn't look at me the way she used to. She's just paper, I can tell." Out of the corner of my eye, I noticed a museum guard come walking through a little wooden door, half hidden behind a screen. I knew that it must lead to the other part of the museum, the part that had the Secrets of the Nile exhibition in it. And suddenly I found myself taking a step toward the door. I felt as if there was something prodding me on. I wasn't sure if it was the priestess's ancient power working its spell on me again, or if it was just my own curiosity and need to finally put all this mummy business to rest. Whatever it was, I knew I needed to go through that door.

"Where are you going?" Keg cried, grabbing my arm.

"If we go through that door, we might be able to find out what happened to the priestess's *ka*," I told him as I took another step toward the door. "Don't you want to know where it is?"

"Not really," he groaned. "And besides, I don't think we're supposed to leave the gallery."

"We'll come right back," I told him, pulling him along with me. Together we made our way over to the door. When no one was looking, I reached out for the brass doorknob and turned it. Then I quickly slipped through the door with Keg close behind.

Suddenly we found ourselves in one of the rooms of the Egyptian exhibit. The stillness of the place made me feel like I was in a funeral home. Nothing moved, nothing stirred. All the display lights were off. And without their soft, warm glow, everything seemed so dead. Old and dead, I was thinking, as I took one little step at a time.

Keg was hanging on to me, as spooked as I was. With each step, I had to drag him along. "We shouldn't be in here alone," he was muttering. "We really shouldn't."

"Sh . . ." I whispered. "Look, there's the tomb."

"Don't make me go in." Keg's voice was growing higher and higher. "I don't want to go in."

"It's the only way we can know if the priestess's *ka* has returned. Besides I want to say thank you."

"Thank you, for what?" Keg cried.

"For a lot of things."

Keg groaned at this and shut his eyes. "I can't go in," he moaned. "Just tell her thank you and I'll wait out here."

"Don't be such a baby," I told him as I took another step. "We've got to go in."

"I can't look," he muttered. "Tell me when we're there."

"All right, here we go." I was hoping to sound calm, but my voice had become as quavery as Keg's. I took a step into the tomb, pulling Keg by the arm as I went. As frightened as I was, I felt I had to keep going even though I was shaking so badly that my teeth began clicking in my head. We walked past the long gray panels carved with falcons and ancient hieroglyphs.

"We're . . . here," I managed to stutter as we stood before the long glass display case. I noticed at once that the overhead lights were off. It was difficult to make out the ancient form lying in the shadows of the case.

"Hurry, up," Keg whimpered, his eyes still shut tight. "Will you hurry up so we can get out of here?" I was about to look down into the case, when my courage suddenly failed me and I shut my eyes tight.

"I just wanted to say thank you," I managed to mumble, "for all the wishes. And for making my life so magnificent," I sputtered. Then I slowly opened my eyes and peeked down into the glass case to see the carved face of the mummy. I searched for some sign of life, but could find none. The stiff wooden features revealed nothing.

"I don't think her *ka* came back," I whispered, pulling on Keg's sleeve. "Look for yourself."

"I'm not looking at anything in here," Keg said, refusing to open his eyes. "And if the priestess's *ka* decided not to come back here, I think she's got the right idea. This is no place to be hanging out in. It's too creepy."

"But if the priestess's *ka* didn't return here, then where is it?" I wondered aloud. Before Keg could answer me, we heard the unmistakable sound of footsteps outside the tomb.

"There it is!" Keg gulped. "It's the *ka,* and it's come to get us!"

CHAPTER EIGHTEEN

"I could have sworn I saw some kids sneak in here," a low voice muttered. Keg and I ducked down low behind the display case and shut our eyes tight. The *ka* was walking, and talking, and who knew what else!

"It's just my luck to have to work this Saturday," the voice continued to grumble. "I'll probably spend the whole morning running around checking on all these kids."

"The *ka* hates kids! We're dead! We're dead!" Keg whimpered.

"But that can't be the *ka*," I whispered.

"Why not?"

"Because the *ka* is a spirit and spirits don't work."

"All right, you two, come on out of there," the voice suddenly boomed, as a flash of light shone in our eyes. Slowly we stood up to see an old red-faced museum guard standing before us. He was waving his flashlight and shaking his head.

"You aren't supposed to be in here. Don't you know that the museum doesn't open until twelve this afternoon?" he growled. "The only room open now is the Children's Gallery." We lowered our heads and followed him back out to the gallery, relieved that he hadn't been a vengeful *ka* after all. But as we stepped back out into the brightly lit room, I couldn't help wondering about the priestess's *ka*. If it had left my paper mummy and hadn't returned to the priestess, then where was it? I knew it had to be somewhere in the museum.

"Here they are!" Marie called out on seeing us.

"We've been looking all over for you two," Dad said, taking my arm. "Jason was showing us his boat, and we wanted you two to show us your projects." Keg's family joined us and together we all went over to see my mummy first. As everyone stood admiring her, I found myself staring into those blue eyes of hers. And even though I couldn't feel her looking back, as she once had, I found myself talking to her anyway.

"I hope the priestess's *ka* comes to rest in a good place," I whispered under my breath before walking away. Then we all followed Keg as he walked toward his project.

" 'Wiley's Mummy'?" His sister Megan read aloud the bold black lettering across the little, sand-colored pyramid. "Why did you call it Wiley's Mummy?" she wanted to know. Keg shifted nervously from foot to foot.

"It's kind of in honor of your Wiley, since he just died and all." Keg shot me a look, and I shook my head. I couldn't believe he hadn't told them yet.

"But the little mummy," Keg's mother was saying as she peered into the tomb. "Is that supposed to be Meg's hamster?"

Keg nodded. "That's who it's supposed to be."

Everyone took a turn looking into the tomb through the eyeholes that Keg had cut into the pyramid.

"It shows a great deal of originality," Mrs. Foley was saying as she stood, looking in.

"Mrs. Foley," Keg's dad called. "Could we get a picture of you and Keg standing by his pyramid?" Mrs. Foley nodded her head and smiled. Then Mr. McGrath took a picture of Mrs. Foley with Keg and his tomb.

"Mrs. Foley, if you wouldn't mind," Marie said, coming up beside her, "could we get a picture of you with our boys and their projects, too." Mrs. Foley smiled a big smile, as if she were a movie star. Marie took lots of pictures. Then they took a walk around the room, looking at all the other projects. Keg and I went back to Wiley's tomb. We both leaned over toward the pyramid, and with one eye each, we peeked inside.

"He really looks great," I told Keg.

"Yeah, he's one great little mummy," Keg said with a grin. Then without warning, the little mummy moved! As we stood staring into the peepholes, Keg and I watched as the perfectly wrapped Wiley began to gently rock back and forth!

"I see it, but I don't believe it," Keg whispered. We lifted our heads up to see Jason standing on the other side of the pyramid. He had a funny smile on his face as he walked away. Had he shaken the pyramid? Or had the little mummy moved all by itself?

"Do you think it was Jason shaking the pyramid?" Keg whispered.

"Maybe," I whispered back. "Or maybe it was the priestess's *ka*. Maybe it found a new resting place." We both bent down and looked back in the tomb.

Later, as Keg and I followed our families out of the museum, Keg turned around for one last look.

"Good old Wiley," he whispered. "Who would have thought he would have ended up so . . . ?"

"So magnificent," I finished his sentence for him and we both began to laugh.

A Note to the Reader

When the ancient Egyptians first invented their written language they used pictures. The pictures were then used to represent sounds. These symbols were called hieroglyphs. They were carved into stone thousands of years ago.

After this ancient way of writing died out in Egypt, those who understood the meaning of the hieroglyphs died, too. For over a thousand years, modern man was unable to decipher the meaning of these early symbols. An entire language was locked in mystery. Then in 1799 archaeologists working in Egypt uncovered the Rosetta Stone, a stone tablet inscribed with a decree of Ptolemy V in Greek, Egyptian hieroglyphic, and Demotic. Twenty-three years later, a young Frenchman, Jean-François Champollion broke the code and was the first person in our time to read and understand the ancient hieroglyphs. With this discovery, modern man was able to reach back through time and listen to the voices of those who had been silenced for centuries.

Melissa Kulp and Melissa Good
with their magnificent mummy

ABOUT THE AUTHOR

As Elvira Woodruff travels around the country visiting schools, she collects artwork done by students. On a recent trip to an elementary school in Bedminster, Pennsylvania, she discovered some magnificent mummy paintings hanging in the hallway outside a fifth-grade classroom. One mummy in particular captured her attention. After meeting with the two young artists who created it, Ms. Woodruff offered to swap some of her books for their painting. That mummy was the inspiration for this book, and today, it hangs in her kitchen, where it continues to be a source of inspiration for all who see it.

Ms. Woodruff has written many popular middle-grade novels, including *The Summer I Shrunk My Grandmother*; *Dear Napoleon, I Know You're Dead, But . . .*; and *George Washington's Socks* (Scholastic Hardcover). Formerly a storyteller in a library, Ms. Woodruff now makes her living as a full-time writer in Martin's Creek, Pennsylvania, where she lives with her two sons.

GET
Goosebumps
by R.L. Stine

☐ BAB45365-3	#1	Welcome to Dead House	$3.99
☐ BAB45369-6	#5	The Curse of the Mummy's Tomb	$3.99
☐ BAB49445-7	#10	The Ghost Next Door	$3.99
☐ BAB49450-3	#15	You Can't Scare Me!	$3.99
☐ BAB47742-0	#20	The Scarecrow Walks at Midnight	$3.99
☐ BAB48355-2	#25	Attack of the Mutant	$3.99
☐ BAB48350-1	#26	My Hairiest Adventure	$3.99
☐ BAB48351-X	#27	A Night in Terror Tower	$3.99
☐ BAB48352-8	#28	The Cuckoo Clock of Doom	$3.99
☐ BAB48347-1	#29	Monster Blood III	$3.99
☐ BAB48348-X	#30	It Came from Beneath the Sink	$3.99
☐ BAB48349-8	#31	The Night of the Living Dummy II	$3.99
☐ BAB48344-7	#32	The Barking Ghost	$3.99
☐ BAB48345-5	#33	The Horror at Camp Jellyjam	$3.99
☐ BAB48346-3	#34	Revenge of the Lawn Gnomes	$3.99
☐ BAB48340-4	#35	A Shocker on Shock Street	$3.99
☐ BAB56873-6	#36	The Haunted Mask II	$3.99
☐ BAB56874-4	#37	The Headless Ghost	$3.99
☐ BAB56875-2	#38	The Abominable Snowman of Pasedena	$3.99
☐ BAB56676-0	#39	How I Got My Shrunken Head	$3.99
☐ BAB56877-9	#40	Night of the Living Dummy III	$3.99
☐ BAB56878-7	#41	Bad Hare Day	$3.99
☐ BAB56879-5	#42	Egg Monsters from Mars	$3.99

Scare me, thrill me, mail me GOOSEBUMPS Now!

Available wherever you buy books, or use this order form. Scholastic Inc., P.O. Box 7502, 2931 East McCarty Street, Jefferson City, MO 65102

Please send me the books I have checked above. I am enclosing $_____ (please add $2.00 to cover shipping and handling). Send check or money order — no cash or C.O.D.s please.

Name _____ Age _____

Address_____

City_____ State/Zip _____

Please allow four to six weeks for delivery. Offer good in the U.S. only. Sorry, mail orders are not available to residents of Canada. Prices subject to change.

If chilling out is your favorite thing to do, you'll love

The Dollhouse Murders
by Betty Ren Wright

Christina's Ghost
by Betty Ren Wright

A Ghost in the House
by Betty Ren Wright

Ghosts Beneath Our Feet
by Betty Ren Wright

The Magnificent Mummy Maker
by Elvira Woodruff

The Girl in the Window
by Wilma Yeo

Scared Stiff
by Jahnna Malcolm

Scared to Death
by Jahnna Malcolm

Terrifying tales of suspense to read all summer long. Look for the day-glo cobwebs on the cover of each book—available this July at bookstores everywhere.